# The Tinder Box

MINETTE WALTERS

# The Tinder Box

PAN BOOKS

First published in Dutch 1999 by De Boekerij bv, Amsterdam

First published in English 1999 in *Ellery Queen Mystery Magazine*, New York

First published in Great Britain 2004 by Macmillan

This paperback edition first published 2005 by Pan Books
an imprint of Pan Macmillan Ltd
Pan Macmillan, 20 New Wharf Road, London N1 9RR
Basingstoke and Oxford
Associated companies throughout the world
www.panmacmillan.com

ISBN 0 330 43850 6

A CIP catalogue record for this book is available from
the British Library.

Typeset by SetSystems Ltd, Saffron Walden, Essex
Printed and bound in Great Britain by
Mackays of Chatham plc, Chatham, Kent

*For our god-daughters*

*Holly, Laura and Olivia*

## Author's Note

In 1998 CPNB, the Organization for the Promotion of Books in the Netherlands, invited me to write a promotional suspense novella for the 1999 Book Week. I called the story *The Tinder Box* and it first appeared in Dutch translation under the title *De Tondeldoos*. I was already working on ideas for my next novel, *Acid Row*, and I took the opportunity of the novella to explore themes of prejudice, incitement and vigilantism that would re-occur in the novel. *The Tinder Box* portrays immigrant Irish tinkers as hate figures in a wealthy Hampshire village, but a similar hatred is demonstrated against a convicted paedophile in a sink estate in *Acid Row*. Both stories depict the dangers of ignorance, and how unrelated, misunderstood events combine to trigger violent reactions. Re-reading *The Tinder Box* for this publication, I was struck by how little human nature changes. When I conceived the idea for the plot, the Good Friday Peace Accord had just been signed, and the people of these islands were optimistic that terrorism was at an end. How quickly that optimism was dashed when the twenty-first century exploded in flames across our television screens.

**Minette Walters**

## Sowerbridge Village

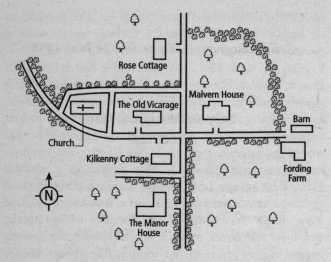

Rose Cottage

Malvern House

The Old Vicarage

Barn

Church

Kilkenny Cottage

Fording Farm

N

The Manor House

# One

Daily Telegraph – *Wednesday, 24 June 1998*

## Sowerbridge Man Arrested

Patrick O'Riordan, 35, an unemployed Irish labourer, was charged last night with the double murder of his neighbours Lavinia Fanshaw, 93, and her live-in nurse, Dorothy Jenkins, 67. The murders have angered the small community of Sowerbridge, where O'Riordan and his parents have lived for fifteen years. The elderly victims were brutally battered to death after Dorothy Jenkins interrupted a robbery on Saturday night. 'Whoever killed them is a monster,' said a neighbour. 'Lavinia was a frail old lady with Alzheimer's who never hurt a soul.' Police warned residents to remain calm after a crowd gathered outside the O'Riordan home when news of the arrest became public. 'Vigilante behaviour will not be tolerated,' said a spokesman. O'Riordan denies the charges.

### Monday, 8 March 1999, 11.30 p.m.

Even at half past eleven at night, the lead news story on local radio was still the opening day of Patrick O'Riordan's trial. Siobhan Lavenham, exhausted after a fourteen-hour stint at work, listened to it in the darkness of her car while she negotiated the narrow country lanes back to Sowerbridge village.

'*O'Riordan smiled as the prosecution case unfolded . . . harrowing details of how ninety-three-year-old Lavinia Fanshaw and her live-in nurse were brutally bludgeoned to death before Mrs Fanshaw's rings were ripped from her fingers . . . scratch marks and bruises on the defendant's face, probably caused by a fight with one of the women . . . a crime of greed triggered by O'Riordan's known resentment of Mrs Fanshaw's wealth . . . unable to account for his whereabouts at the time of the murders . . . items of jewellery recovered from the O'Riordan family home which the thirty-five-year-old Irishman still shares with his elderly parents . . .*'

With a sinking heart, Siobhan punched the Off button and concentrated on her driving. '*The Irishman . . .*' Was that a deliberate attempt to inflame racist division, she wondered, or just careless shorthand? God, how she loathed journalists! Confident of a guilty verdict, they had descended on Sowerbridge like a plague of locusts the previous week in order to prepare their background features in advance. They had found dirt in abundance, of course. Sowerbridge had fallen over itself to feed them with hate stories against the whole O'Riordan family.

She thought back to the day of Patrick's arrest, when Bridey, his mother, had begged her not to abandon them. 'You're one of us, Siobhan. Irish through and through, never mind you're married to an Englishman. You know my Patrick. He wouldn't hurt a fly. Is it likely he'd beat Mrs Fanshaw to death when he's never raised a hand against his own father? Liam was a devil when he still had the use of his arm. Many's the time he thrashed Patrick with a stick when the drunken rages were on him, but never once did Patrick take the stick to him.'

It was a frightening thing to be reminded of the bonds that tied people together, Siobhan had thought as she looked out of Bridey's window towards the silent, angry crowd that was gathering in the road. Was being Irish enough of a reason to side with a man suspected of slaughtering a frail bedridden old woman and the woman who looked after her?

'Patrick admits he stole from Lavinia,' Siobhan had pointed out.

Tears rolled down Bridey's furrowed cheeks. 'But not her rings,' she said. 'Just cheap trinkets that he was too ignorant to recognize as worthless paste.'

'It was still theft.'

'Mother of God, do you think I don't know that?'

She held out her hands beseechingly. 'A thief he may be, Siobhan, but never a murderer.'

And Siobhan had believed her because she wanted to. For all his sins, she had never thought of Patrick as an aggressive or malicious man – too relaxed by half, many would say – and he could always make her and her children laugh with his stories about Ireland, particularly ones involving leprechauns and pots of gold hidden at the ends of rainbows. The thought of him taking a hammer to anyone was anathema to her.

*And yet . . .?*

In the darkness of the car she recalled the interview she'd had the previous month with a detective inspector at Hampshire Constabulary Headquarters, who seemed perplexed that a well-to-do young woman should have sought him out to complain about police indifference to the plight of the O'Riordans. She wondered now why she hadn't gone to him sooner.

*Had she really been so unwilling to learn the truth . . .?*

*Wednesday, 10 February 1999*

The detective shook his head. 'I don't understand what you're talking about, Mrs Lavenham.'

Siobhan gave an angry sigh. 'Oh, for goodness sake! The hate campaign that's being waged against them. The graffiti on their walls, the constant telephone calls threatening them with arson, the fact that Bridey's too frightened to go out for fear of being attacked. There's a war going on in Sowerbridge which is getting worse the closer we come to Patrick's trial, but as far as you're concerned it doesn't exist. Why aren't you investigating it? Why don't you respond to Bridey's telephone calls?'

He consulted a piece of paper on his desk. 'Mrs O'Riordan's made fifty-three emergency calls in the eight months since Patrick was remanded for the murders,' he said, 'only thirty of which were considered serious enough to send a police car to investigate. In every case, the attending officers filed reports saying Bridey was wasting police time.' He gave an apologetic shrug. 'I realize it's not what you want to hear, but we'd be within our rights if we decided to prosecute her. Wasting police time is a serious offence.'

Siobhan thought of the tiny, wheelchair-bound

woman whose terror was so real she trembled constantly. 'They're after killing us, Siobhan,' she would say over and over again. 'I hear them creeping about the garden in the middle of the night and I think to myself, there's nothing me or Liam can do if this is the night they decide to break in. To be sure, it's only God who's keeping us safe.'

'But who *are* they, Bridey?'

'It's the bully boys whipped up to hate us by Mrs Haversley and Mr Jardine,' wept the woman. 'Who else would it be?'

Siobhan brushed her long dark hair from her forehead and frowned at the detective inspector. 'Bridey's old, she's disabled, and she's completely terrified. The phone never stops ringing. Mostly it's long silences, other times it's voices threatening to kill her. Liam's only answer to it all is to get paralytically drunk every night so he doesn't have to face up to what's going on.' She shook her head impatiently. 'Cynthia Haversley and Jeremy Jardine, who seem to control everything that happens in Sowerbridge, have effectively given carte blanche to the local youths to make life hell for them. Every sound, every shadow has Bridey on the edge of her seat. She needs protection, and I don't understand why you're not giving it to her.'

'They were offered a safe house, Mrs Lavenham, and they refused it.'

'Because Liam's afraid of what will happen to Kilkenny Cottage if he leaves it empty,' she protested.

'The place will be trashed in half a minute flat . . . You know that as well as I do.'

He gave another shrug, this time more indifferent than apologetic. 'I'm sorry,' he said, 'but there's nothing we can do. If any of these attacks actually happened . . . well, we'd have something concrete to investigate. They can't even name any of these so-called vigilantes . . . just claim they're yobs from neighbouring villages.'

'So what are you saying?' she asked bitterly. 'That they have to be dead before you take the threats against them seriously?'

'Of course not,' he said, 'but we do need to be persuaded the threats are real. As things stand, they seem to be all in her mind.'

'Are you accusing Bridey of lying?'

He smiled slightly. 'She's never been averse to embroidering the truth when it suits her purpose, Mrs Lavenham.'

Siobhan shook her head. 'How can you say that? Have you ever spoken to her? Do you even *know* her? To you, she's just the mother of a thief and a murderer.'

'That's neither fair nor true.' He looked infinitely weary, like a defendant in a trial who has answered the same accusation in the same way a hundred times before. 'I've known Bridey for years. It's part and parcel of being a policeman. When you question a man as often as I've questioned Liam, you get to know his wife pretty well by default.' He leaned forward, resting his elbows on his knees and clasping his hands loosely in front of him. 'And sadly, the one sure thing I know about Bridey is that you can't believe a word she says. It may not be her fault, but it *is* a fact. She's never had the courage to speak out honestly because her drunken brute of a husband beats her within an inch of her life if she even dares to think about it.'

Siobhan found his directness shocking. 'You're talking about things that happened a long time ago,' she said. 'Liam hasn't struck anyone since he lost the use of his right arm.'

'Do you know how that happened?'

'In a car crash.'

'Did Bridey tell you that?'

'Yes.'

'Not so,' he countered bluntly. 'When Patrick was twenty, he tied Liam's arm to a table top and used a hammer to smash his wrist to a pulp. He was so wrought up that when his mother tried to stop him, he shoved her through a window and broke her pelvis so badly she's never been able to walk again. That's why she's in a wheelchair and why Liam has a useless right arm. Patrick got off lightly by pleading provocation because of Liam's past brutality towards him, and spent less than two years in prison for it.'

Siobhan shook her head. 'I don't believe you.'

'It's true.' He rubbed a tired hand around his face. 'Trust me, Mrs Lavenham.'

'I can't,' she said flatly. 'You've never lived in

Sowerbridge, Inspector. There's not a soul in that village who doesn't have it in for the O'Riordans and a juicy titbit like that would have been repeated a thousand times. Trust *me*.'

'No one knows about it.' The man held her gaze for a moment, then dropped his eyes. 'It was fifteen years ago and it happened in London. I was a raw recruit with the Met, and Liam was on our ten-most-wanted list. He was a scrap-metal merchant, and up to his neck in villainy, until Patrick scuppered him for good. He sold up when the lad went to prison and moved himself and Bridey down here to start a new life. When Patrick joined them after his release, the story of the car crash had already been accepted.'

She shook her head again. 'Patrick came over from Ireland after being wounded by a terrorist bomb. That's why he smiles all the time. The nerves in his cheek were severed by a piece of flying glass.' She sighed. 'It's another kind of disability. People take against him because they think he's laughing at them.'

'No, ma'am, it was a revenge attack in prison for stealing from his cellmate. His face was slashed with a razor. As far as I know, he's never set foot in Ireland.'

She didn't answer. Instead she ran her hand rhythmically over her skirt while she tried to collect her thoughts. *Oh, Bridey, Bridey, Bridey . . . Have you been lying to me . . .?*

The inspector watched her with compassion. 'Nothing happens in a vacuum, Mrs Lavenham.'

'Meaning what, exactly?'

'Meaning that Patrick murdered Mrs Fanshaw –' he paused – 'and both Liam and Bridey know he did. You can argue that the physical abuse he suffered at the hands of his father as a child provoked an anger in him that he couldn't control – it's a defence that worked after the attack on Liam – but it won't cut much ice with a jury when the victims were two defenceless old ladies. That's why Bridey's jumping at shadows. She knows that she effectively signed Mrs Fanshaw's death warrant when she chose to keep quiet about how dangerous Patrick was, and she's terrified of it becoming public.' He paused. 'Which it certainly will during the trial.'

Was he right, Siobhan wondered? Were Bridey's fears rooted in guilt? 'That doesn't absolve the police of responsibility for their safety,' she pointed out.

'No,' he agreed, 'except we don't believe their safety's in question. Frankly, all the evidence so far points to Liam himself being the instigator of the hate campaign. The graffiti is always done at night in car spray paint, at least a hundred cans of which are stored in Liam's shed. There are never any witnesses to it, and by the time Bridey calls us the perpetrators are long gone. We've no idea if the phone rings as constantly as they claim, but on every occasion that a threat has been made Bridey admits she was alone in the cottage. We think Liam is making the calls himself.'

She shook her head in bewilderment. 'Why would he do that?'

'To prejudice the trial?' he suggested. 'He has a different mindset to you and me, ma'am, and he's quite capable of trashing Kilkenny Cottage himself if he thinks it will win Patrick some sympathy with a jury.'

Did she believe him? Was Liam that clever? 'You said you were always questioning him. Why? What had he done?'

'Any scam involving cars. Theft. Forging MOT certificates. Odometer fixing. You name it, Liam was involved in it. The scrap-metal business was just a front for a car-laundering operation.'

'You're talking about when he was in London?'

'Yes.'

She pondered for a moment. 'Did he go to prison for it?'

'Once or twice. Most of the time he managed to avoid conviction. He had money in those days – a lot of money – and could pay top briefs to get him off. He shipped some of the cars down here, presumably with the intention of starting the same game again, but he was a broken man after Patrick smashed his arm. I'm told he gave up grafting for himself and took to living off disability benefit instead. There's no way anyone was going to employ him. He's too unreliable to hold down a job. Just like his son.'

'I see,' said Siobhan slowly.

He waited for her to go on, and when she didn't he said, 'Leopards don't change their spots, Mrs Lavenham. I wish I could say they did, but I've been a policeman too long to believe anything so naive.'

She surprised him by laughing. 'Leopards?' she echoed. 'And there was me thinking we were talking about dogs.'

'I don't follow.'

'Give a dog a bad name and hang him. Did the police *ever* intend to let them wipe the slate clean and start again, Inspector?'

He smiled slightly. 'We did . . . for fifteen years . . . Then Patrick murdered Mrs Fanshaw.'

'Are you sure?'

'Oh, yes,' he said. 'He used the same hammer on her that he used on his father.'

Siobhan remembered the sense of shock that had swept through the village the previous June when the two bodies were discovered by the paper boy after his curiosity had been piqued by the fact that the front door had been standing ajar at six thirty on a Sunday morning. Thereafter, only the police and Lavinia's grandson had seen inside the house, but the rumour machine described a scene of carnage, with Lavinia's brains splattered across the walls of her bedroom and her nurse lying in a pool of blood in the kitchen. It was inconceivable that anyone in Sowerbridge could have done such a thing, and it was assumed the Manor House had been targeted by an outside gang for whatever valuables the old woman might possess.

It was never very clear why police suspicion had centred so rapidly on Patrick O'Riordan. Gossip said his fingerprints were all over the house and his toolbox was found in the kitchen, but Siobhan had always believed the police had received a tipoff. Whatever the reason, the matter appeared to be settled when a search warrant unearthed Lavinia's jewellery under his floorboards and Patrick was formally charged with the murders.

Predictably, shock had turned to fury but, with Patrick already in custody, it was Liam and Bridey who took the full brunt of Sowerbridge's wrath. Their presence in the village had never been a particularly welcome one – indeed, it was a mystery how 'rough trade like them' could have afforded to buy a cottage in rural Hampshire, or why they had wanted to – but they became deeply unwelcome after the murders. Had it been possible to banish them behind a physical pale, the village would most certainly have done so; as it was, the old couple were left to exist in a social limbo where backs were turned and no one spoke to them.

In such a climate, Siobhan wondered, could Liam really have been stupid enough to ratchet up the hatred against them by daubing anti-Irish slogans across his front wall?

'If Patrick *is* the murderer, then why didn't you find Lavinia's diamond rings in Kilkenny Cottage?' she asked the inspector. 'Why did you only find pieces of fake jewellery?'

'Who told you that? Bridey?'

'Yes.'

He looked at her with a kind of compassion. 'Then I'm afraid she was lying, Mrs Lavenham. The diamond rings were in Kilkenny Cottage along with everything else.'

# Two

*Monday, 8 March 1999, 11.45 p.m.*

Siobhan was aware of the orange glow in the night sky ahead of her for some time before her tired brain began to question what it meant. Arc lights? A party? Fire, she thought in alarm as she approached the outskirts of Sowerbridge and saw sparks shooting into the air like a giant Roman candle. She slowed her Range Rover to a crawl as she approached the bend by the church, knowing it must be the O'Riordans' house, tempted to put the car into reverse and drive away, as if denial could alter what was happening. But she could see the flames licking up the front of Kilkenny Cottage by that time and knew it was too late for anything so simplistic. A police car was blocking the narrow road ahead, and with a sense of foreboding she obeyed the torch that signalled her to draw up on the grass verge beyond the church gate.

She lowered her window as the policeman came over, and felt the warmth from the fire fan her face like a Saharan wind. 'Do you live in Sowerbridge, madam?' he asked. He was dressed in shirtsleeves, perspiration glistening on his forehead, and Siobhan was amazed that one small house two hundred yards away could generate so much heat on a cool March night.

'Yes.' She gestured in the direction of the blaze. 'At Fording Farm. It's another half-mile beyond the crossroads.'

He shone his torch into her eyes for a moment – his curiosity whetted by her soft Dublin accent, she guessed – before lowering the beam to a map. 'You'll waste a lot less time if you go back the way you came and make a detour,' he advised her.

'I can't. Our driveway leads off the crossroads by Kilkenny Cottage and there's no other access to it.' She touched a finger to the map. 'There. Whichever way I go, I still need to come back to the crossroads.'

Headlights swept across her rearview mirror as another car rounded the bend. 'Wait there a moment, please.' He moved away to signal towards the verge, leaving Siobhan to gaze through her windscreen at the scene of chaos ahead.

There seemed to be a lot of people milling around, but her night sight had been damaged by the brilliance of the flames; and the water glistening on the tarmac made it difficult to distinguish what was real from what was reflection. The rusted hulks of the old cars that littered the O'Riordans' property stood out in bold silhouettes against the light, and Siobhan thought that Cynthia Haversley had been right when she said they weren't just an eyesore but a fire hazard as well. Cynthia had talked dramatically about the dangers of petrol, but if there was any petrol left in the corroded tanks, it remained sluggishly inert. The real hazard was the time and effort it must have taken to manoeuvre the two fire engines close enough to weave the hoses through so many obstacles, and Siobhan wondered if the house had ever stood a chance of being saved.

She began to fret about her two small boys and their nanny, Rosheen, who were alone at the farmhouse, and drummed her fingers impatiently on the steering wheel. 'What should I do?' she asked the policeman when he returned after persuading the other driver to make a detour. 'I need to get home.'

He looked at the map again. 'There's a footpath running behind the church and the vicarage. If you're prepared to walk home, I suggest you park your car in the churchyard and take the footpath. I'll radio through to ask one of the constables on the other side of the crossroads to escort you into your driveway. Failing that, I'm afraid you'll have to stay here until the road's clear, and that could take several hours.'

'I'll walk.' She reached for the gear stick, then let her hand drop. 'No one's been hurt, have they?'

'No. The occupants are away.'

Siobhan nodded. Under the watchful eyes of half of Sowerbridge village Liam and Bridey had set off that morning in their ancient Ford estate, to the malignant sound of whistles and hisses. 'The

O'Riordans are staying in Winchester until the trial's over.'

'So we've been told,' the policeman agreed.

Siobhan watched him take a notebook from his breast pocket. 'Then presumably you were expecting something like this? I mean, everyone knew the house would be empty.'

He flicked to an empty page. 'I'll need your name, madam.'

'Siobhan Lavenham.'

'And your registration number, please, Ms Lavenham.'

She gave it to him. 'You didn't answer my question,' she said unemphatically.

He raised his eyes to look at her but it was impossible to read their expression. 'What question's that?'

She thought she detected a smile on his face and bridled immediately. 'You don't find it at all suspicious that the house burns down the minute Liam's back is turned?'

He frowned. 'You've lost me, Ms Lavenham.'

'It's *Mrs* Lavenham,' she said irritably, 'and you know perfectly well what I'm talking about. Liam's been receiving arson threats ever since Patrick was arrested, but the police couldn't have been less interested.' Her irritation got the better of her. 'It's their son who's on trial, for God's sake, not them, though you'd never believe it for all the care the English police have shown them.' She crunched the car into gear and drove the few yards to the churchyard entrance, where she parked in the lee of the wall and closed the window. She was preparing to open the door when it was opened from the outside.

'What are you trying to say?' demanded the policeman as she climbed out.

'What am I trying to say?' She let her accent slip into broad brogue. 'Will you listen to the man? And there was me thinking my English was as good as his.'

She was as tall as the constable, with striking good looks, and colour rose in his cheeks. 'I didn't mean it that way, Mrs Lavenham. I meant, are you saying it was arson?'

'Of course it was arson,' she countered, securing her mane of brown hair with a band at the back of her neck and raising her coat collar against the wind which two hundred yards away was feeding the inferno. 'Are you saying it wasn't?'

'Can you prove it?'

'I thought that was your job.'

He opened his notebook again, looking more like an earnest student than an officer of the law. 'Do you know who might have been responsible?'

She reached inside the car for her handbag. 'Probably the same people who wrote "IRISH TRASH" across their front wall,' she said, slamming the door and locking it. 'Or maybe it's the ones who broke into the house two weeks ago during the night and smashed Bridey's Madonna and Child before urinating all over the pieces on the carpet. Who knows?'

She gave him credit for looking disturbed at what she was saying. 'Look, forget it,' she said wearily. 'It's late and I'm tired, and I want to get home to my children. Can you make that radio call so I don't get held up at the other end?'

'I'll do it from the car.' He started to turn away, then changed his mind. 'I'll be reporting what you've told me, Mrs Lavenham, including your suggestion that the police have been negligent in their duty.'

She smiled slightly. 'Is that a threat or a promise, Officer?'

'It's a promise.'

'Then I hope you have better luck than I've had. I might have been speaking in Gaelic for all the notice your colleagues took of my warnings.' She set off for the footpath.

'You're supposed to put complaints in writing,' he called after her.

'Oh, but I did,' she assured him over her shoulder. 'I may be Irish, but I'm not illiterate.'

'I didn't mean—'

But the rest of his apology was lost on her as she rounded the corner of the church and vanished from sight.

*Thursday, 18 February 1999*

It had been several days before Siobhan found the courage to confront Bridey with what the detective inspector had told her. It made her feel like a thief even to think about it. Secrets were such fragile things. Little parts of oneself that couldn't be exposed without inviting changed perceptions towards the whole. But distrust was corroding her sympathy and she needed reassurance that Bridey at least believed in Patrick's innocence.

She followed the old woman's wheelchair into the sitting room and perched on the edge of the grubby sofa that Liam always lounged upon in his oil-stained boiler suit after spending hours poking around his unsightly wrecks. It was a mystery to Siobhan what he did, as none of them appeared to be driveable, and she wondered sometimes if he simply used them as a canopy under which to sleep his days away. He complained often enough that his withered right hand, which he kept tucked out of sight inside his pocket, had deprived him of any chance of a livelihood, but the truth was he was a lazy man who was only ever seen to rouse himself when his wife transferred from her wheelchair to the passenger seat of their old Ford.

'There's nothing wrong with his left hand,' Cynthia Haversley would snort indignantly as she watched the regular little pantomime outside Kilkenny Cottage, 'but you'd think he'd lost the use of both hands the way he carries on about his disabilities.'

Privately, and with some amusement, Siobhan guessed the demonstrations were put on entirely for the benefit of the Honourable Mrs Haversley, who made no bones about her irritation at the level of state welfare that the O'Riordans enjoyed. It was axiomatic, after all, that any woman who had enough strength in her arms to heave herself upstairs on her bottom, as Bridey did every night, could lift her own legs into a car . . .

Kilkenny Cottage's sitting room – Bridey called it her 'parlour' – was full of religious artefacts: a shrine to the Madonna and Child on the mantelpiece, a foot-high wooden cross on one wall, a print of William Holman Hunt's *The Light of the World* on another, a rosary hanging from a hook. In Siobhan, for whom religion was more of a trial than a comfort, the room invariably induced a sort of spiritual claustrophobia which made her long to get out and breathe fresh air again.

In ordinary circumstances, the paths of the O'Riordans, descendants of a roaming tinker family, and Siobhan Lavenham (née Kerry), daughter of an Irish landowner, would never have crossed. Indeed, when she and her husband, Ian, first visited Fording Farm and fell in love with it, Siobhan had pointed out the eyesore of Kilkenny Cottage with a shudder and had predicted accurately the kind of people who were living there. Irish gypsies, she'd said.

'Will that make life difficult for you?' Ian had asked.

'Only if people assume we're related,' she answered with a laugh, never assuming for one moment that anyone would . . .

Bridey's habitually cowed expression reminded Siobhan of an ill-treated dog, and she put the detective inspector's accusations reluctantly, asking Bridey if she had lied about the car crash and about Patrick never striking his father. The woman wept, washing her hands in her lap as if, like Lady Macbeth, she could cleanse herself of sin.

'If I did, Siobhan, it was only to have you think well of us. You're a lovely young lady with a kind heart, but you'd not have let Patrick play with your children if you'd known what he did to his father, and you'd not have taken Rosheen into your house if you'd known her uncle Liam was a thief.'

'You should have trusted me, Bridey. If I didn't ask Rosheen to leave when Patrick was arrested for murder, why would I have refused to employ her just because Liam spent time in prison?'

'Because your husband would have persuaded you against her,' said Bridey truthfully. 'He's never been happy about Rosheen being related to us, never mind she grew up in Ireland and hardly knew us till you said she could come here to work for you.'

There was no point denying it. Ian tolerated

Rosheen O'Riordan for Siobhan's sake, and because his little boys loved her, but in an ideal world he would have preferred a nanny from a more conventional background. Rosheen's relaxed attitude to child rearing, based on her own upbringing in a three-bedroomed cottage in the hills of Donegal, where the children had slept four to a bed and play was adventurous, carefree, and fun, was so different from the strict supervision of his own childhood that he constantly worried about it. 'They'll grow up wild,' he would say. 'She's not disciplining them enough.' And Siobhan would look at her happy, lively, affectionate sons and wonder why the English were so fond of repression.

'He worries about his children, Bridey, more so since Patrick's arrest. We get telephone calls too, you know. Everyone knows Rosheen's his cousin.'

She remembered the first such call she had taken. She had answered it in the kitchen while Rosheen was making supper for the children, and she had been shocked by the torrent of anti-Irish abuse that had poured down the line. She raised stricken eyes to Rosheen's and saw by the girl's frightened expression that it wasn't the first such call that had been made. After that, she had had an answerphone installed, and forbade Rosheen to lift the receiver unless she was sure of the caller's identity.

Bridey's sad gaze lifted towards the Madonna on the mantelpiece. 'I pray for you every day, Siobhan, just as I pray for my Patrick. God knows, I never wished this trouble on a sweet lady such as yourself. And for why? Is it a sin to be Irish?'

Siobhan sighed to herself, hating Bridey's dreary insistence on calling her a 'lady'. She did not doubt Bridey's faith, nor that she prayed every day, but she doubted God's ability to undo Lavinia Fanshaw's murder eight months after the event.

*And if Patrick was guilty of it, and Bridey knew he was guilty...*

'The issue isn't about being Irish,' she said bluntly, 'it's about whether or not Patrick's a murderer. I'd much rather you were honest with me, Bridey. At the moment, I don't trust any of you, and that includes Rosheen. Does she know about his past? Has she been lying to me too?' She paused, waiting for an answer, but Bridey just shook her head. 'I'm not going to blame you for your son's behaviour,' she said more gently, 'but you can't expect me to go on pleading his cause if he's guilty.'

'Indeed, and I wouldn't ask you to,' said the old woman with dignity. 'And you can rest your mind about Rosheen. We kept the truth to ourselves fifteen years ago. Liam wouldn't have his son blamed for something that wasn't his fault. We'll call it a car accident, he said, and may God strike me dead if I ever raise my hand in anger again.' She grasped the rims of her chair wheels and slowly rotated them through half a turn. 'I'll tell you honestly, though I'm a cripple and though I've been married to Liam for nearly forty years, it's only in these last fifteen that

I've been able to sleep peacefully in my bed. Oh yes, Liam was a bad man, and oh yes, my Patrick lost his temper once and struck out at him, but I swear by the Mother of God that this family changed for the better the day my poor son wept for what he'd done and rang the police himself. Will you believe me, Siobhan? Will you trust an old woman when she tells you her Patrick could no more have murdered Mrs Fanshaw than I can get out of this wheelchair and walk? To be sure, he took some jewellery from her – and to be sure, he was wrong to do it – but he was only trying to get back what had been cheated out of him.'

'Except there's no proof he was cheated out of anything. The police say there's very little evidence that any odd jobs had been done in the manor. They mentioned that one or two cracks in the plaster had been filled, but not enough to indicate a contract worth three hundred pounds.'

'He was up there for two weeks,' said Bridey in despair. 'Twelve hours a day every day.'

'Then why is there nothing to show for it?'

'I don't know,' said the old woman with difficulty. 'All I can tell you is that he came home every night with stories about what he'd been doing. One day it was getting the heating system to work, the next re-laying the floor tiles in the kitchen where they'd come loose. It was Miss Jenkins who was telling him what needed doing, and she was thrilled to have all the little irritations sorted once and for all.'

Siobhan recalled the detective inspector's words.

'*There's no one left to agree or disagree,*' he had said. '*Mrs Fanshaw's grandson denies knowing anything about it, although he admits there might have been a private arrangement between Patrick and the nurse. She's known to have been on friendly terms with him . . .*'

'The police are saying Patrick only invented the contract in order to explain why his fingerprints were all over the Manor House.'

'That's not true.'

'Are you sure? Wasn't it the first idea that came into his head when the police produced the search warrant? They questioned him for two days, Bridey, and the only explanation he gave for his fingerprints and his toolbox being in the manor was that Lavinia's nurse had asked him to sort out the dripping taps in the kitchen and bathroom. Why didn't he mention a contract earlier? Why did he wait until they found the jewellery under his floorboards before saying he was owed money?'

Teardrops watered the washing hands. 'Because he's been in prison and doesn't trust the police . . . because he didn't kill Mrs Fanshaw . . . because he was more worried about being charged with the theft of her jewellery than he was about being charged with murder. Do you think he'd have invented a contract that didn't exist? My boy isn't stupid, Siobhan. He doesn't tell stories that he can't back up. Not when he's had two whole days to think about them.'

Siobhan shook her head. 'Except he couldn't back it up. You're the only person, other than Patrick, who claims to know anything about it, and your word means nothing because you're his mother.'

'But don't you see?' the woman pleaded. 'That's why you can be sure Patrick's telling the truth. If he'd believed for one moment it would all be denied, he'd have given some other reason for why he took the jewellery. Do you hear what I'm saying? He's a good liar, Siobhan – for his sins, he always has been – and he'd not have invented a poor, weak story like the one he's been saddled with.'

# Three

It was a rambling defence that Patrick finally produced when it dawned on him that the police were serious about charging him with the murders. Siobhan heard both Bridey's and the inspector's versions of it, and she wasn't surprised that the police found it difficult to swallow. It depended almost entirely on the words and actions of the murdered nurse.

Patrick claimed Dorothy Jenkins had come to Kilkenny Cottage and asked him if he was willing to do some odd jobs at the Manor House for a cash sum of three hundred pounds. 'I've finally persuaded her miserable skinflint of a grandson that I'll walk out one day and not come back if he doesn't do something about my working conditions, so he's agreed to pay up,' she had said triumphantly. 'Are you interested, Patrick? It's a bit of moonlighting . . . no VAT . . . no tax . . . just a couple of weeks' work for money in hand. For goodness sake don't go talking about it,' she had warned him, 'or you can be sure Cynthia

Haversley will notify social services that you're working and you'll lose your unemployment benefit. You know what an interfering busybody she is.'

'I needed convincing she wasn't pulling a fast one,' Patrick told the police. 'I've been warned off in the past by that bastard grandson of Mrs F's and the whole thing seemed bloody unlikely to me. So she takes me along to see him, and he's nice as pie, shakes me by the hand and says it's a kosher contract. "We'll let bygones be bygones," he says. I worked like a dog for two weeks and, yes, of course I went into Mrs Fanshaw's bedroom. I popped in every morning because she and I were mates. I would say "hi," and she would giggle and say "hi" back. And yes, I touched almost everything in the house – most of the time I was moving furniture around for Miss Jenkins. "It's so boring when you get too old to change things," she'd say to me. "Let's see how that table looks in here." Then she'd clap her hands and say, "Isn't this exciting?" I thought she was almost as barmy as the old lady, but I wasn't going to argue with her. I mean, three hundred quid is three hundred quid, and if that's what was wanted I was happy to do the business.'

On the second Saturday – 'the day I was supposed to be paid . . . shit . . . I should have known it was a scam . . .' – Mrs Fanshaw's grandson was in the hall waiting for him when he arrived at the Manor House.

'I thought the bastard had come to give me my wages, but instead he accuses me of nicking a necklace. I called him a bloody liar, so he took a swing at me and landed one on my jaw. Next thing I know, I'm out of the front door, face down on the gravel. Yeah, of course that's how I got the scratches. I've never hit a woman in my life, and I certainly didn't get into a fight with either of the old biddies at the manor.'

There was a two-hour hiatus during which he claimed to have driven around in a fury wondering how 'to get the bastard to pay what he owed'. He toyed with the idea of going to the police – 'I was pretty sure Miss Jenkins would back me up, she was that mad with him, but I didn't reckon you lot could do anything, not without social services getting to hear about it, and then I'd be worse off than I was before . . .' – but in the end he opted for more direct action and sneaked back to the manor through the gate at the bottom of the garden.

'I knew Miss Jenkins would see me right if she could. And she did. "Take this, Patrick," she said, handing me some of Mrs F's jewellery, "and if there's any comeback I'll say it was my idea." I tell you,' he finished aggressively, 'I'm gutted she and Mrs F are dead. At least they treated me like a friend, which is more than can be said of the rest of Sowerbridge.'

He was asked why he hadn't mentioned any of this before. 'Because I'm not a fool,' he said. 'Word has it Mrs F was killed for her jewellery. Do you think I'm going to admit to having some of it under my floor-boards when she was battered to death a few hours later?'

*Thursday, 18 February 1999*

Siobhan pondered in silence for a minute or two. 'Weak or not, Bridey, it's the story he has to go to trial with, and at the moment no one believes it. It would be different if he could prove any of it.'

'How?'

'I don't know.' She shook her head. 'Did he show the jewellery to anyone *before* Lavinia was killed?'

A sly expression crept into the woman's eyes as if a new idea had suddenly occurred to her. 'Only to me and Rosheen,' she said, 'but, as you know, Siobhan, not a word we say is believed.'

'Did either of you mention it to anyone else?'

'Why would we? When all's said and done, he took the things without permission, never mind it was Miss Jenkins who gave them to him.'

'Well, it's a pity Rosheen didn't tell me about it. It would make a world of difference if I could say I knew on the Saturday afternoon that Patrick already had Lavinia's rings and necklace in his possession.'

Bridey looked away towards her Madonna, crossing herself as she did so, and Siobhan knew she was lying. 'She thinks the world of you, Siobhan. She'd not embarrass you by making you a party to her cousin's troubles. In any case, you'd not have been interested.

Was your mind not taken up with cooking that day? Was that not the Saturday you were entertaining Mr and Mrs Haversley to dinner to pay off all the dinners you've had from them but never wanted?'

There were no secrets in a village, thought Siobhan, and if Bridey knew how much Ian and she detested the grinding tedium of Sowerbridge social life, which revolved around the all-too-regular 'dinner party', presumably the rest of Sowerbridge did as well. 'Are we really that obvious, Bridey?'

'To the Irish, maybe, but not to the English,' said the old woman with a crooked smile. 'The English see what they want to see. If you don't believe me, Siobhan, look at the way they've condemned my Patrick as a murdering thief before he's even been tried.'

Siobhan had questioned Rosheen about the jewellery afterwards and, like Bridey, the girl had wrung her hands in distress. But Rosheen's distress had everything to do with her aunt expecting her to perjure herself and nothing at all to do with the facts. 'Oh, Siobhan,' she had wailed, 'does she expect me to stand up in court and tell lies? Because it'll not do Patrick any good when they find me out. Surely it's better to say nothing than to keep inventing stories that no one believes?'

### Monday, 8 March 1999, 11.55 p.m.

It was cold on the footpath because the wall of the Old Vicarage was reflecting the heat back towards Kilkenny Cottage, but the sound of the burning house was deafening. The pine rafters and ceiling joists popped and exploded like intermittent rifle fire while the flames kept up a hungry roar. As Siobhan emerged onto the road leading up from the junction, she found herself in a crowd of her neighbours who seemed to be watching the blaze in a spirit of revelry – almost, she thought in amazement, as if it were a spectacular fireworks display put on for their enjoyment. People raised their arms and pointed whenever a new rafter caught alight, and 'oohs' and 'ahs' burst from their mouths like a cheer. Any moment now, she thought cynically, and they'd bring out an effigy of that other infamous Catholic, Guy Fawkes.

She started to work her way through the crowd but was stopped by Nora Bentley, the elderly doctor's wife, who caught her arm and drew her close. The Bentleys were far and away Siobhan's favourites among her neighbours, being the only ones with enough tolerance to stand against the continuous barrage of anti-O'Riordan hatred that poured from the mouths of almost everyone else. Although, as Ian often pointed out, they could afford to be tolerant. 'Be fair, Siobhan. Lavinia wasn't related to them. They might feel differently if she'd been *their* granny.'

'We've been worried about you, my dear,' said Nora. 'What with all this going on, we didn't know whether you were trapped inside the farm or outside.'

Siobhan gave her a quick hug. 'Outside. I stayed late at work to sort out some contracts, and I've had to abandon the car at the church.'

'Well, I'm afraid your drive's completely blocked with fire engines. If it's any consolation, we're all in the same boat, although Jeremy Jardine and the Haversleys have the added worry of sparks carrying on the wind and setting light to their houses.' She chuckled suddenly. 'You have to laugh. Cynthia bullied the firemen into taking preventative measures by hosing down the front of Malvern House, and now she's tearing strips off poor old Peter because he left their bedroom window open. The whole room's completely saturated.'

Siobhan grinned. 'Good,' she said, unsympathetically. 'It's time Cynthia had some of her own medicine.'

Nora wagged an admonishing finger. 'Don't be too hard on her, my dear. For all her sins, Cynthia can be very kind when she wants to be. It's a pity you've never seen that side of her.'

'I'm not sure I'd want to,' said Siobhan cynically. 'At a guess, she only shows it when she's offering charity. Where are they, anyway?'

'I've no idea. I expect Peter's making up the spare-room beds and Cynthia's at the front somewhere behaving like the chief constable. You know how bossy she is.'

'Yes,' agreed Siobhan, who had been on the receiving end of Cynthia's hectoring tongue more often than she cared to remember. Indeed, if she had any regrets about moving to Sowerbridge, they were all centred around the overbearing personality of the Honourable Mrs Haversley.

By one of those legal quirks of which the English are so fond, the owners of Malvern House had title to the first hundred feet of Fording Farm's driveway while the owners of the farm had right of way in perpetuity across it. This had led to a state of war between the two households, although it was a war that had been going on long before the Lavenhams' insignificant tenure of eighteen months. Ian maintained that Cynthia's insistence on her rights stemmed from the fact that the Haversleys were, and always had been, the poor relations of the Fanshaws at the Manor House. ('You get slowly more impoverished if you inherit through the distaff side,' he said, 'and Peter's family has never been able to lay claim to the manor. It's made Cynthia bitter.') Nevertheless, had he and Siobhan paid heed to their solicitor's warnings, they might have questioned why such a beautiful place had had five different owners in under ten years. Instead, they had accepted the previous owners' assurances that everything in the garden was lovely – *You'll like*

*Cynthia Haversley. She's a charming woman* – and put the rapid turnover down to coincidence.

Something that sounded like a grenade detonating exploded in the heart of the fire and Nora Bentley jumped. She tapped her heart with a fluttery hand. 'Goodness me, it's just like the war,' she said in a rush. '*So* exciting.' She tempered this surprising statement by adding that she felt sorry for the O'Riordans, but it was clear her sympathy came a poor second to her desire for sensation.

'Are Liam and Bridey here?' asked Siobhan, looking around.

'I don't think so, dear. To be honest, I wonder if they even know what's happening. They were very secretive about where they were staying in Winchester; unless the police know where they are, well –' she shrugged – 'who could have told them?'

'Rosheen knows.'

Nora gave an absent-minded smile. 'Yes, but she's with your boys at the farm.'

'We are on the phone, Nora.'

'I know, dear, but it's all been so sudden. One minute, nothing – the next, mayhem. As a matter of fact, I did suggest we call Rosheen, but Cynthia said there was no point. Let Liam and Bridey have a good night's sleep, she said. What can they do that the fire brigade haven't already done? Why bother them unnecessarily?'

'I'll bear that in mind when Cynthia's house goes up in flames,' said Siobhan dryly, glancing at her watch and telling herself to get a move on. Curiosity held her back. 'When did it start?'

'No one knows,' said Nora. 'Sam and I smelt burning about an hour and a half ago and came to investigate, but by that time the flames were already at the downstairs windows.' She waved an arm at the Old Vicarage. 'We knocked up Jeremy and got him to call the fire brigade, but the whole thing was out of control long before they arrived.'

Siobhan's eyes followed the waving arm. 'Why didn't Jeremy call them earlier? Surely he'd have smelt burning before you did? He lives right opposite.' Her glance travelled on to the Bentleys' house, Rose Cottage, which stood behind the Old Vicarage, a good hundred yards distant from Kilkenny Cottage.

Nora looked anxious, as if she, too, found Jeremy Jardine's inertia suspicious. 'He says he didn't, says he was in his cellar. He was horrified when he saw what was going on.'

Siobhan took that last sentence with a pinch of salt. Jeremy Jardine was a wine shipper who had used his Fanshaw family connection some years before to buy the Old Vicarage off the church commissioners for its extensive cellars. But the beautiful brick house looked out over the O'Riordans' unsightly wrecking ground, and he was one of their most strident critics. No one knew how much he'd paid for it, although rumour suggested it had been sold off at a fifth of its value. Certainly questions had been asked at the time about why a substantial Victorian house had never been advertised for sale on the open market, although, as usual in Sowerbridge, answers were difficult to come by when they involved the Fanshaw family.

Prior to the murders, Siobhan had been irritated enough by Jeremy's unremitting criticism of the O'Riordans to ask him why he'd bought the Old Vicarage, knowing what the view was going to be. 'It's not as though you didn't know about Liam's cars,' she told him. 'Nora Bentley says you'd been living with Lavinia at the manor for two years before the purchase.'

Jeremy had muttered darkly about good investments turning sour when promises of action failed to materialize and Siobhan had interpreted this as meaning he'd paid a pittance to acquire the property from the church on the mistaken understanding that one of his district councillor buddies could force the O'Riordans to clean up their frontage.

Ian had laughed when she told him about the conversation. 'Why on earth doesn't he just offer to pay for the clean-up himself? Liam's never going to pay to have those blasted wrecks removed, but he'd be pleased as punch if someone else did.'

'Perhaps he can't afford it. Nora says the Fanshaws aren't half as well off as everyone believes, and Jeremy's business is no great shakes. I know he talks grandly about how he supplies all the top families with quality wine, but that case he sold us was rubbish.'

'It wouldn't cost much, not if a scrap-metal merchant did it.'

Siobhan had wagged a finger at him. 'You know what your problem is, husband of mine? You're too sensible to live in Sowerbridge. Also, you're ignoring the fact that there's an issue of principle at stake. If Jeremy pays for the clean-up then the O'Riordans will have won. Worse still, they will be seen to have won because *their* house will also rise in value the minute the wrecks go.'

He shook his head. 'Just promise me you won't start taking sides, Shiv. You're no keener on the O'Riordans than anyone else, and there's no law that says the Irish have to stick together. Life's too short to get involved in their ridiculous feuds.'

'I promise,' she had said, and at the time she had meant it.

But that was before Patrick had been charged with murder . . .

There was no doubt in the minds of most of Sowerbridge's inhabitants that Patrick O'Riordan saw Lavinia Fanshaw as an easy target. In November, two years previously, he had relieved the confused old woman of a Chippendale chair worth five hundred pounds after claiming a European directive required all hedgerows to be clipped to a uniform standard. He had stripped her laurels to within four feet of the ground in return for the antique, and had sold the foliage on to a crony who made festive Christmas wreaths.

Nor had he shown any remorse. 'It was a bit of business,' he said in the pub afterwards, grinning happily as he swilled his beer, 'and she was pleased as punch about it. She told me she's always hated that chair.' He was a small, wiry man with a shock of dark hair and penetrating blue eyes which stared unwaveringly at the person he was talking to – like a fighting dog whose intention was to intimidate. 'In any case, I did this village a favour. The manor looks a damn sight better since I sorted the frontage.'

The fact that most people agreed with him was neither here nor there. The combination of Lavinia's senility and extraordinary longevity meant the Manor House was rapidly falling into disrepair, but this did not entitle anyone, least of all an O'Riordan, to take advantage of her. What about Kilkenny Cottage's frontage? people protested. Liam's cars were a great deal worse than Lavinia's overgrown hedge. There was even suspicion that her live-in nurse had connived in the fraud because she was known to be extremely critical of the deteriorating conditions in which she was expected to work.

'I can't be watching Mrs Fanshaw twenty-four hours a day,' Dorothy Jenkins had said firmly, 'and if she makes an arrangement behind my back, then there's nothing I can do about it. It's her grandson you should be talking to. He's the one with power of attorney over her affairs, but he's never going to sell this place before she's dead because he's too mean to put her in a nursing home. She could live forever the way she's going, and nursing homes cost far more than I do. He pays me peanuts because he says I'm getting free board and lodging, but there's no heating, the roof leaks, and the whole place is a death trap of rotten floorboards. He's only waiting for the poor old thing to die so that he can sell the land to a property developer and live in clover for the rest of his life.'

## Monday, 8 March 1999, midnight

The crowd seemed to be growing bigger and more boisterous by the minute, but as Siobhan recognized few of the faces, she realized word of the fire must have spread to surrounding villages. She couldn't understand why the police were letting thrill-seekers through until she heard someone say that he'd parked on the Southampton Road and cut across a field to bypass the police block. There was much jostling for position; the smell of beer on the breath of one man who pushed past her was overpowering. He barged against her and she jabbed him angrily in the ribs with a sharp elbow before taking Nora's arm and shepherding her across the road.

'People are going to be hurt in a minute,' she said. 'They've obviously come straight from the pub.' She manoeuvred through a knot of people beside the wall of Malvern House, and ahead of her she saw Nora's husband, Dr Sam Bentley, talking with Peter and Cynthia Haversley. 'There's Sam. I'll leave you with him and then be on my way. I'm worried about Rosheen and the boys.' She nodded briefly to the Haversleys, raised a hand in greeting to Sam Bentley, then prepared to push on.

'You won't get through,' said Cynthia forcefully,

planting her corseted body between Siobhan and the crossroads. 'They've barricaded the entire junction, and no one's allowed past.' Her face had turned crimson from the heat, and Siobhan wondered if she had any idea how unattractive she looked. The combination of dyed blonde hair atop a glistening beetroot complexion was reminiscent of sherry trifle, and Siobhan wished she had a camera to record the fact. Siobhan knew Cynthia to be in her late sixties because Nora had let slip once that she and Cynthia shared a birthday, but Cynthia herself preferred to draw a discreet veil over her age. Privately (and rather grudgingly) Siobhan admitted she had a case because her plumpness gave her skin a smooth, firm quality which made her look considerably younger than her years, although it didn't make her any more likeable.

Siobhan had asked Ian once if he thought her anti-pathy to Cynthia was an 'Irish thing'. The idea had amused him. 'On what basis? Because the Honourable Mrs Haversley symbolizes colonial authority?'

'Something like that.'

'Don't be absurd, Shiv. She's a fat snob with a power complex who loves throwing her weight around. No one likes her. *I* certainly don't. She probably wouldn't be so bad if her wet husband had ever stood up to her, but poor old Peter's as cowed as everyone else. You should learn to ignore her. In the great scheme of things, she's about as relevant as birdshit on your windscreen.'

'I *hate* birdshit on my windscreen.'

'I know,' he had said with a grin, 'but you don't assume pigeons single your car out because you're Irish, do you?'

She made an effort now to summon a pleasant smile as she answered Cynthia. 'Oh, I'm sure they'll make an exception of me. Ian's in Italy this week, which means Rosheen and the boys are on their own. I think I'll be allowed through in the circumstances.'

'If you aren't,' said Dr Bentley, 'Peter and I can give you a leg-up over the wall and you can cut through Malvern House garden.'

'Thank you.' She studied his face for a moment. 'Does anyone know how the fire started, Sam?'

'We think Liam must have left a cigarette burning.'

Siobhan pulled a wry face. 'Then it must have been the slowest-burning cigarette in history,' she said. 'They were gone by nine o'clock this morning.'

He looked as worried as his wife had done earlier. 'It's only a guess.'

'Oh, come on! If it was a smouldering cigarette you'd have seen flames at the windows by lunchtime.' She turned her attention back to Cynthia. 'I'm surprised that Sam and Nora smelt burning before you did,' she said with deliberate lightness. 'You and Peter are so much closer than they are.'

'We probably would have done if we'd been here,' said Cynthia, 'but we went to supper with friends in Salisbury. We didn't get home until after Jeremy called the fire brigade.' She stared Siobhan down, daring her to dispute the statement.

'Matter of fact,' said Peter, 'we only just scraped in before the police arrived with barricades. Otherwise they'd have made us leave the car at the church.'

Siobhan wondered if the friends had invited the Haversleys or if the Haversleys had invited themselves. She guessed the latter. None of the O'Riordans' neighbours would have wanted to save Kilkenny Cottage, and unlike Jeremy, she thought sarcastically, the Haversleys had no cellar to skulk in. 'I really must go,' she said then. 'Poor Rosheen will be worried sick.' But if she expected sympathy for Liam and Bridey's niece, she didn't get it.

'If she were *that* worried, she'd have come down here,' declared Cynthia. 'With or without your boys. I don't know why you employ her. She's one of the laziest and most deceitful creatures I've ever met. Frankly, I wouldn't have her for love or money.'

Siobhan smiled slightly. It was like listening to a cracked record, she thought. The day the Honourable Mrs Haversley resisted an opportunity to snipe at an O'Riordan would be a red-letter day in Siobhan's book. 'I suspect the feeling's mutual, Cynthia. Threat of death might persuade her to work for you, but not love or money.'

Cynthia's retort, a pithy one if her annoyed expression was anything to go by, was swallowed by the sound of Kilkenny Cottage collapsing inwards upon itself as the beams supporting the roof finally gave way. There was a shout of approval from the crowd behind them, and while everyone else's attention was temporarily distracted, Siobhan watched Peter Haversley give his wife a surreptitious pat on the back.

# Four

Siobhan had stubbornly kept an open mind about Patrick's guilt, although as she was honest enough to admit to Ian, it was more for Rosheen and Bridey's sake than because she seriously believed there was room for reasonable doubt. She couldn't forget the fear she had seen in Rosheen's eyes one day when she came home early to find Jeremy Jardine at the front door of the farm. 'What are you doing here?' she had demanded of him angrily, appalled by the ashen colour in her nanny's cheeks.

There was a telling silence before Rosheen stumbled into words.

'He says we're murdering Mrs Fanshaw all over again by taking Patrick's side,' said the girl in a shaken voice. 'I said it was wrong to condemn him before the evidence is heard – you told me everyone would believe Patrick was innocent until the trial – but Mr Jardine just keeps shouting at me.'

Jeremy had laughed. 'I'm doing the rounds with

my new wine list,' he said, jerking his thumb towards his car. 'But I'm damned if I'll stay quiet while an Irish murderer's cousin quotes English law at me.'

Siobhan had controlled her temper because her two sons were watching from the kitchen window. 'Go inside now,' she told Rosheen, 'but if Mr Jardine comes here again when Ian and I are at work, I want you to phone the police immediately.' She waited while the girl retreated with relief into the depths of the house. 'I mean it, Jeremy,' she said coldly. 'However strongly you may feel about all of this, I'll have you prosecuted if you try that trick again. It's not as though Rosheen has any evidence that can help Patrick, so you're simply wasting your time.'

He shrugged. 'You're a fool, Siobhan. Patrick's guilty as sin. You know it. Everyone knows it. Just don't come crying to me later when the jury proves us right and you find yourself tarred with the same brush as the O'Riordans.'

'I already have been,' she said curtly. 'If you and the Haversleys had your way, I'd have been lynched by now, but, God knows, I'd give my right arm to see Patrick get off, if only to watch the three of you wearing sackcloth and ashes for the rest of your lives.'

Ian had listened to her account of the conversation with a worried frown on his face. 'It won't help Patrick if he does get off,' he warned. 'No one's going to believe he didn't do it. Reasonable doubt sounds all very well in court, but it won't count for anything in Sowerbridge. He'll never be able to come back.'

'I know.'

'Then don't get too openly involved,' he advised. 'We'll be living here for the foreseeable future, and I really don't want the boys growing up in an atmosphere of hostility. Support Bridey and Rosheen by all means – ' he gave her a wry smile – 'but do me a favour, Shiv, and hold that Irish temper of yours in check. I'm not convinced Patrick is worth going to war over, particularly not with our close neighbours.'

It was good advice, but difficult to follow. There was too much overt prejudice against the Irish in general for Siobhan to stay quiet indefinitely. War finally broke out at one of Cynthia and Peter Haversley's tedious dinner parties at Malvern House, which were impossible to avoid without telling so many lies that it was easier to attend the wretched things. 'She watches the driveway from her window,' sighed Siobhan when Ian asked why they couldn't just say they had another engagement that night. 'She keeps tabs on everything we do. She knows when we're in and when we're out. It's like living in a prison.'

'I don't know why she keeps inviting us,' he said.

Siobhan found his genuine ignorance of Cynthia's motives amusing. 'It's her favourite sport,' she said matter-of-factly. 'Bear-baiting . . . with me as the bear.'

Ian sighed. 'Then let's tell her the truth, say we'd rather stay in and watch television.'

'Good idea. There's the phone. *You* tell her.'

He smiled unhappily. 'It'll make her even more impossible.'

'Of course it will.'

'Perhaps we should just grit our teeth and go?'

'Why not? It's what we usually do.'

The evening had been a particularly dire one, with Cynthia and Jeremy holding the platform as usual, Peter getting quietly drunk, and the Bentleys making only occasional remarks. A silence had developed round the table and Siobhan, who had been firmly biting her tongue since they arrived, consulted her watch under cover of her napkin and wondered if nine forty-five was too early to announce departure.

'I suppose what troubles me the most,' said Jeremy suddenly, 'is that if I'd pushed to have the O'Riordans evicted years ago, poor old Lavinia would still be alive.' He was a similar age to the Lavenhams and handsome in a florid sort of way – *too much sampling of his own wares*, Siobhan always thought – and loved to style himself as Hampshire's most eligible bachelor. Many was the time Siobhan had wanted to ask why, if he was so eligible, he remained unattached, but she didn't bother because she thought she knew the answer. He couldn't find a woman stupid enough to agree with his own valuation of himself.

'You can't evict people from their own homes,' Sam Bentley pointed out mildly. 'On that basis, we could all be evicted any time our neighbours took against us.'

'Oh, you know what I mean,' Jeremy answered,

looking pointedly at Siobhan as if to remind her of his warning about being tarred with the O'Riordans' brush. 'There must be something I could have done – had them prosecuted for environmental pollution, perhaps?'

'We should never have allowed them to come here in the first place,' declared Cynthia. 'It's iniquitous that the rest of us have no say over what sort of people will be living on our doorsteps. If the Parish Council was allowed to vet prospective newcomers, the problem would never have arisen.'

Siobhan raised her head and smiled in amused disbelief at the other woman's arrogant assumption that the Parish Council was in her pocket. 'What a good idea!' she said brightly, ignoring Ian's frown across the table. 'It would also give prospective newcomers a chance to vet the people already living here. It means house prices would drop like a stone, of course, but at least neither side could say afterwards that they went into it with their eyes closed.'

The pity was that Cynthia was too stupid to understand irony. 'You're quite wrong, my dear,' she said with a condescending smile. 'The house prices would go *up*. They always do when an area becomes exclusive.'

'Only when there are enough purchasers who want the kind of exclusivity you're offering them, Cynthia. It's basic economics.' Siobhan propped her elbows on the table and leaned forward, stung into pricking the fat woman's self-righteous bubble once and for all, even if she did recognize that her real target was Jeremy Jardine. 'And for what it's worth, there won't be any competition to live in Sowerbridge when word gets out that, *however* much money you have, there's no point in applying unless you share the Fanshaw mafia's belief that Hitler was right.'

Nora Bentley gave a small gasp and made damping gestures with her hands.

Jeremy was less restrained. 'Well, my God!' he burst out aggressively. 'That's bloody rich coming from an Irishwoman. Where was Ireland in the war? Sitting on the sidelines, rooting for Germany, that's where. And you have the damn nerve to sit in judgement on us! All you Irish are despicable. You flood over here like a plague of sewer rats looking for handouts, then you criticize us when we point out that we don't think you're worth the trouble you're causing us.'

It was like a simmering saucepan boiling over. In the end, all that had been achieved by restraint was to allow resentment to fester. On both sides.

'I suggest you withdraw those remarks, Jeremy,' said Ian coldly, rousing himself in defence of his wife. 'You might be entitled to insult Siobhan like that if your business paid as much tax and employed as many people as hers does, but as that's never going to happen I think you should apologize.'

'No way. Not unless she apologizes to Cynthia first.'

Once roused, Ian's temper was even more volatile than his wife's. 'She's got nothing to apologize for,' he snapped. 'Everything she said was true. Neither you nor Cynthia has any more right than anyone else to dictate what goes on in this village, yet you do it anyway. And with very little justification. At least the rest of us bought our houses fair and square on the open market, which is more than can be said of you or Peter. He inherited his, and you got yours cheap via the old-boy network. I just hope you're prepared for the consequences when something goes wrong. You can't incite hatred and then pretend you're not responsible for it.'

'Now, now, now!' said Sam with fussy concern. 'This sort of talk isn't healthy.'

'Sam's right,' said Nora. 'What's said can never be unsaid.'

Ian shrugged. 'Then tell this village to keep its collective mouth shut about the Irish in general and the O'Riordans in particular. Or doesn't the rule apply to them? Perhaps it's only the well-to-do English like the Haversleys and Jeremy who can't be criticized?'

Peter Haversley gave an unexpected snigger. 'Well-to-do?' he muttered tipsily. 'Who's well-to-do? We're all in hock up to our blasted eyeballs while we wait for the manor to be sold.'

'Be quiet, Peter,' said his wife.

But he refused to be silenced. 'That's the trouble with murder. Everything gets so damned messy. You're not allowed to sell what's rightfully yours because probate goes into limbo.' His bleary eyes looked across the table at Jeremy. 'It's your fault, you sanctimonious little toad. Power of bloody attorney, my arse. You're too damn greedy for your own good. Always were . . . always will be. I kept telling you to put the old bloodsucker into a home but would you listen? Don't worry, you kept saying, she'll be dead soon . . .'

### Tuesday, 9 March 1999, 0.23 a.m.

The hall lights were on in the farmhouse when Siobhan finally reached it, but there was no sign of Rosheen. This surprised her until she checked the time and saw that it was well after midnight. She went into the kitchen and squatted down to stroke Patch, the O'Riordans' amiable mongrel, who lifted his head from the hearth in front of the Aga and wagged his stumpy tail before giving an enormous yawn and returning to his slumbers. Siobhan had agreed to look after him while the O'Riordans were away and he seemed entirely at home in his new surroundings. She peered out of the kitchen window towards the fire, but there was nothing to see except the dark line of trees bordering the property, and it occurred to her then that Rosheen probably had no idea her uncle's house had gone up in flames.

She tiptoed upstairs to check on her two young sons who, like Patch, woke briefly to wrap their arms around her neck and acknowledge her kisses before closing their eyes again. She paused outside Rosheen's room for a moment, hoping to hear the sound of the girl's television, but there was only silence and she retreated downstairs again, relieved to be spared explanations tonight. Rosheen had been frightened enough by the anti-Irish slogans daubed across the front of Kilkenny Cottage; God only knew how she would react to hearing it had been destroyed.

Rosheen's employment with them had happened more by accident than design when Siobhan's previous nanny – a young woman given to melodrama – had announced after two weeks in rural Hampshire that she'd rather 'die' than spend another night away from the lights of London. In desperation, Siobhan had taken up Bridey's shy suggestion to fly Rosheen over from Ireland on a month's trial – '*She's Liam's brother's daughter and she's a wonder with children. She's been looking after her brothers and cousins since she was knee-high to a grasshopper, and they all think the world of her*' – and Siobhan had been surprised by how quickly and naturally the girl had fitted into the household.

Ian had reservations – '*She's too young – she's too scatter-brained . . . I'm not sure I want to be quite so cosy with the O'Riordans*' – but he had come to respect her in the wake of Patrick's arrest when, despite the hostility in the village, she had refused to abandon either Siobhan or Bridey. 'Mind you, I wouldn't bet on family loyalty being what's keeping her here.'

'What else is there?'

'Sex with Kevin Wyllie. She goes weak at the knees every time she sees him, never mind he's probably intimately acquainted with the thugs who're terrorizing Liam and Bridey.'

'You can't blame him for that. He's lived here all

his life. I should imagine most of Sowerbridge could name names if they wanted to. At least he's had the guts to stand by Rosheen.'

'He's an illiterate oaf with an IQ of ten,' growled Ian. 'Rosheen's not stupid, so what the hell do they find to talk about?'

Siobhan giggled. 'I don't think his conversation is what interests her.'

Recognizing that she was too hyped-up to sleep, she poured herself a glass of wine and played the messages on the answerphone. There were a couple of business calls followed by one from Ian. *'Hi, it's me. Things are progressing well on the Ravenelli front. All being well, hand-printed Italian silk should be on offer through Lavenham Interiors by August. Good news, eh? I can think of at least two projects that will benefit from the designs they've been showing me. You'll love them, Shiv. Aquamarine swirls with every shade of terracotta you can imagine.'* Pause for a yawn. *'I'm missing you and the boys like crazy. Give me a ring if you get back before eleven, otherwise I'll speak to you tomorrow. I should be home on Friday.'* He finished with a slobbery kiss which made her laugh.

The last message was from Liam O'Riordan and had obviously been intercepted by Rosheen. *'Hello? Are you there, Rosheen? It's . . .'* said Liam's voice before it was cut off by the receiver being lifted. Out of curiosity, Siobhan pressed one-four-seven-one to find out when Liam had phoned, and she listened in perplexity as the computerized voice at the other end gave the time of the last call as 'twenty thirty-six hours', and the number from which it was made as 'eight-two-seven-five-three-eight'. She knew the sequence off by heart but flicked through the telephone index anyway to make certain. *Liam and Bridey O'Riordan, Kilkenny Cottage, Sowerbridge, Tel: 827538.*

For the second time that night her first instinct was to rush towards denial. It was a mistake, she told herself . . . Liam couldn't possibly have been phoning from Kilkenny Cottage at eight thirty . . . The O'Riordans were under police protection in Winchester for the duration of Patrick's trial . . . Kilkenny Cottage was empty when the fire started . . .

*But, oh dear God! Supposing it wasn't?*

'Rosheen!' she shouted, running up the stairs again and hammering on the nanny's door. 'Rosheen! It's Siobhan. Wake up! Was Liam in the cottage?' She thrust open the door and switched on the light, only to look around the room in dismay because no one was there.

## Wednesday, 10 February 1999

Siobhan had raised the question of Lavinia Fanshaw's heirs with the detective inspector. 'You can't ignore the fact that both Peter Haversley and Jeremy Jardine had a far stronger motive than Patrick could ever have had,' she pointed out. 'They both stood to inherit from her will, and neither of them made any bones about wanting her dead. Lavinia's husband had one sister, now dead, who produced a single child, Peter, who has *no* children. And Lavinia's only child, a daughter, also dead, produced Jeremy, who's never married.'

He was amused by the extent of her research. 'We didn't ignore it, Mrs Lavenham. It was the first thing we looked at, but you know better than anyone that they couldn't have done it because you and your husband supplied their alibis.'

'Only from eight o'clock on Saturday night until two o'clock on Sunday morning,' protested Siobhan. 'And not out of choice either. Have you any idea what it's like living in a village like Sowerbridge, Inspector? Dinner parties are considered intrinsically superior to staying in of a Friday or Saturday night and watching telly, never mind the same boring people get invited every time and the same boring conversations take place. It's a status thing.' She gave a sarcastic shrug. 'Personally, I'd rather watch a good Arnie or Sly movie any day than have to appear interested in someone else's mortgage or pension plan, but then – *hell* – I'm Irish and everyone knows the Irish are common as muck.'

'You'll have status enough when Patrick comes to trial,' said the inspector with amusement. 'You'll be the one providing the alibis.'

'I wouldn't be able to if we'd managed to get rid of Jeremy and the Haversleys any sooner. Believe me, it wasn't Ian and I who kept them there – we did everything we could to make them go – they just refused to take the hints. Sam and Nora Bentley went at a reasonable time, but we couldn't get the rest of them to budge. Are you *sure* Lavinia was killed between eleven and midnight? Don't you find it suspicious that it's *my* evidence that's excluded Peter and Jeremy from the case? Everyone knows I'm the only person in Sowerbridge who'd give Patrick O'Riordan an alibi if I possibly could.'

'What difference does that make?'

'It means I'm a reluctant witness, and therefore gives my evidence in Peter and Jeremy's favour more weight.'

The inspector shook his head. 'I think you're making too much of your position in all of this, Mrs Lavenham. If Mr Haversley and Mr Jardine had conspired to murder Mrs Fanshaw, wouldn't they have taken themselves to – say, Ireland – for the weekend?

That would have given them a much stronger alibi than spending six hours in the home of a hostile witness. In any case,' he went on apologetically, 'we are sure about the time of the murders. These days, pathologists' timings are extremely precise, particularly when the bodies are found as quickly as these ones were.'

Siobhan wasn't ready to give up so easily. 'But you must see how odd it is that it happened the night Ian and I gave a dinner party. We *hate* dinner parties. Most of our entertaining is done around barbecues in the summer when friends come to stay. It's always casual and always spur-of-the-moment and I can't believe it was coincidence that Lavinia was murdered on the one night in the whole damn year for which we'd sent out invitations – ' her mouth twisted – '*six weeks* in advance . . .'

He eyed her thoughtfully. 'If you can tell me how they did it, I might agree with you.'

'Before they came to our house or after they left it,' she suggested. 'The pathologist's timings are wrong.'

He pulled a piece of paper from a pile on his desk and turned it towards her. 'That's an itemized British Telecom list of every call made from the manor during the week leading up to the murders.' He touched the last number. 'This one was made by Dorothy Jenkins to a friend of hers in London and was timed at ten thirty p.m. on the night she died. The duration time was just over three minutes. We've spoken to the friend and she described Miss Jenkins as at "the end of her tether". Apparently Mrs Fanshaw was a difficult patient to nurse – Alzheimer's sufferers usually are – and Miss Jenkins had phoned this woman – also a nurse – to tell her that she felt like "smothering the old bitch where she lay". It had happened several times before, but this time Miss Jenkins was in tears and rang off abruptly when her friend said she had someone with her and couldn't talk for long.' He paused for a moment. 'The friend was worried enough to phone back after her visitor had gone,' he went on, 'and she estimates the time of that call at about a quarter past midnight. The line was engaged so she couldn't get through, and she admits to being relieved because she thought it meant Miss Jenkins had found someone else to confide in.'

Siobhan frowned. 'Well, at least it proves she was alive after midnight, doesn't it?'

The inspector shook his head. 'I'm afraid not. The phone in the kitchen had been knocked off its rest – we think Miss Jenkins may have been trying to dial nine-nine-nine when she was attacked – ' he tapped his fingers on the piece of paper – 'which means that, with or without the pathologist's timings, she must have been killed between that last itemized call at ten thirty and her friend's return call at fifteen minutes past midnight, when the phone was already off the hook.'

# Five

Even as Siobhan lifted the receiver to call the police and report Rosheen missing, she was having second thoughts. They hadn't taken a blind bit of notice in the past, she thought bitterly, so why should it be different today? She could even predict how the conversation would go simply because she had been there so many times before.

*Calm down, Mrs Lavenham . . . It was undoubtedly a hoax . . . Let's see now . . . didn't someone phone you not so long ago pretending to be Bridey in the throes of a heart attack . . .? We rushed an ambulance to her only to find her alive and well and watching television . . . You and your nanny are Irish . . . Someone thought it would be entertaining to get a rise out of you by creeping into Kilkenny Cottage and making a call . . . Everyone knows the O'Riordans are notoriously careless about locking their back door . . . Sadly we can't legislate for practical jokes . . . Your nanny . . .? She'll be watching the fire along with everyone else . . .*

With a sigh of frustration, she replaced the receiver and listened to the message again. '*Hello? Are you there, Rosheen? It's* . . .'

She had been so sure it was Liam the first time she heard it, but now she was less certain. The Irish accent was the easiest accent in the world to ape, and Liam's was so broad any fool could do it. For want of someone more sensible to talk to, she telephoned Ian in his hotel bedroom in Rome. 'It's me,' she said, 'and I've only just got back. I'm sorry to wake you but they've burnt Kilkenny Cottage and Rosheen's missing. Do you think I should phone the police?'

'Hang on,' he said sleepily. 'Run that one by me again. Who's they?'

'I don't know,' she said in frustration. 'Someone – anyone – Peter Haversley patted Cynthia on the back when the roof caved in. If I knew where the O'Riordans were I'd phone them, but Rosheen's the only one who knows the number – and she's not here. I'd go back to the fire if I had a car – the village is swarming with policemen – but I've had to leave mine at the church and yours is at Heathrow – and the children will never be able to walk all the way down the drive, not at this time of night.'

He gave a long yawn. 'You're going much too fast. I've only just woken up. What's this about Kilkenny Cottage burning down?'

She explained it slowly.

'So where's Rosheen?' He sounded more alert now. 'And what the hell was she doing leaving the boys?'

'I don't know.' She told him about the telephone call from Kilkenny Cottage. 'If it was Liam, Rosheen may have gone up there to see him, and now I'm worried they were in the house when the fire started. Everyone thinks it was empty because we watched them go this morning.' She described the scene for him as Liam helped Bridey into their Ford estate then drove unsmilingly past the group of similarly unsmiling neighbours who had gathered at the crossroads to see them off. 'It was awful,' she said. 'I went down to collect Patch, and bloody Cynthia started hissing at them so the rest joined in. I really hate them, Ian.'

He didn't answer immediately. 'Look,' he said then, 'the fire brigade don't just take people's words for this kind of thing. They'll have checked to make sure there was no one in the house as soon as they got there. And if Liam and Bridey *did* come back, their car would have been parked at the front and someone would have noticed it. OK, I agree the village is full of bigots, but they're not murderers, Shiv, and they wouldn't keep quiet if they thought the O'Riordans were burning to death. Come on, think about it. You know I'm right.'

'What about Rosheen?'

'Yes, well,' he said dryly, 'it wouldn't be the first time, would it? Did you check the barn? I expect she's out there getting laid by Kevin Wyllie.'

'She's only done it once.'

'She's used the barn once,' he corrected her, 'but it's anyone's guess how often she's been laid by Kevin.

66

I'll bet you a pound to a penny they're tucked up together somewhere and she'll come wandering in with a smile on her face when you least expect it. I hope you tear strips off her for it, too. She's no damn business to leave the boys on their own.'

She let it ride, unwilling to be drawn into another argument about Rosheen's morals. Ian worked on the principle that what the eye didn't see the heart didn't grieve over, and refused to recognize the hypocrisy of his position, while Siobhan's view was that Kevin was merely a bit of 'rough' that was keeping Rosheen amused while she looked for something better. *Every woman did it . . . the road to respectability was far from straight*. In any case, she agreed with his final sentiment. Even if it was Liam who had phoned from the cottage, Rosheen's first responsibility was to James and Oliver. 'So what should I do? Just wait for her to come back?'

'I don't see you have much choice. She's over twenty-one so the police won't do anything tonight.'

'OK.'

He knew her too well. 'You don't sound convinced.'

She wasn't, but then she was more relaxed about the way Rosheen conducted herself than he was. The fact that they'd come home early one night and caught her in the barn with her knickers down had offended Ian deeply, even though Rosheen had been monitoring the boys all the time via a two-way transmitter that she'd taken with her. Ian had wanted to sack her on the spot, but Siobhan had persuaded him out of it after extracting a promise from Rosheen that the affair would be confined to her spare time in future. Afterwards, and because she was a great deal less puritanical than her English husband, Siobhan had buried her face in her pillow to stifle her laughter. Her view was that Rosheen had shown typical Irish tact by having sex outside in the barn rather than under the Lavenhams' roof. As she pointed out to Ian: '*We'd never have known Kevin was there if she'd smuggled him into her room and told him to perform quietly.*'

'It's just that I'm tired,' she lied, knowing she could never describe her sense of foreboding down the telephone to someone over a thousand miles away. Empty houses gave her the shivers at the best of times – a throwback to the rambling, echoing mansion of her childhood, which her overactive imagination had peopled with giants and spectres . . . 'Look, go back to sleep and I'll ring you tomorrow. It'll have sorted itself out by then. Just make sure you come home by Friday,' she ended severely, 'or I'll file for divorce immediately. I didn't marry you to be deserted for the Ravenelli brothers.'

'I will,' he promised.

Siobhan listened to the click as he hung up at the other end, then replaced her own receiver before opening the front door and looking towards the dark shape of the barn. She searched for a chink of light between the double doors but knew she was wasting her time even while she was doing it. Rosheen had been so terrified by Ian's threat to tell her parents in Ireland what she'd been up to that her sessions with Kevin were now confined to somewhere a great deal more private than Fording Farm's barn.

With a sigh she retreated to the kitchen and settled on a cushion in front of the Aga with Patch's head lying across her lap and the bottle of wine beside her. It was another ten minutes before she noticed that the key to Kilkenny Cottage, which should have been hanging on a hook on the dresser, was no longer there.

### Wednesday, 10 February 1999

'But why are you so sure it was Patrick?' Siobhan had asked the inspector next. 'Why not a total stranger? I mean, anyone could have taken the hammer from his toolbox if he'd left it in the kitchen the way he says he did.'

'Because there were no signs of a break-in. Whoever killed them either had a key to the front door or was let in by Dorothy Jenkins. And that means it must have been someone she knew.'

'Maybe she hadn't locked up,' said Siobhan, clutching at straws. 'Maybe they came in through the back door.'

'Have you ever tried to open the back door to the manor, Mrs Lavenham?'

'No.'

'Apart from the fact that the bolts were rusted in their sockets, it's so warped and swollen with damp you have to put a shoulder to it to force it ajar, and it screams like a banshee every time you do it. If a stranger had come in through the back door at eleven o'clock at night, he wouldn't have caught Miss Jenkins in the kitchen. She'd have taken to her heels the minute she heard the banshee-wailing and would have used one of the phones upstairs to call the police.'

'You can't know that,' argued Siobhan. 'Sower-bridge is the sleepiest place on earth. Why would she assume it was an intruder? She probably thought it was Jeremy paying a late-night visit to his grand-mother.'

'We don't think so.' He picked up a pen and turned it between his fingers. 'As far as we can establish, that door was never used. Certainly none of the neighbours reported going in that way. The paper boy said Miss Jenkins kept it bolted because on the one occasion when she tried to open it, it became so wedged that she had to ask him to force it shut again.'

She sighed, admitting defeat. 'Patrick's always been so sweet to me and my children. I just can't believe he's a murderer.'

He smiled at her naivety. 'The two are not mutually exclusive, Mrs Lavenham. I expect Jack the Ripper's neighbour said the same about him.'

### Tuesday, 9 March 1999, 1.00 a.m.

People began to shiver as the smouldering remains were dowsed by the fire hoses and the pungent smell of wet ashes stung their nostrils. In the aftermath of excitement, a sense of shame crept among the inhabitants of Sowerbridge – *schadenfreude* was surely alien to their natures? – and bit by bit the crowd began to disperse. Only the Haversleys, the Bentleys and Jeremy Jardine lingered at the crossroads, held by a mutual fascination for the scene of devastation that would greet them every time they emerged from their houses.

'We won't be able to open our windows for weeks,' said Nora Bentley, wrinkling her nose. 'The smell will be suffocating.'

'It'll be worse when the wind gets up and deposits soot all over the place,' complained Peter Haversley, brushing ash from his coat.

His wife clicked her tongue impatiently. 'We'll just have to put up with it,' she said. 'It's hardly the end of the world.'

Sam Bentley surprised her with a sudden bark of laughter. 'Well spoken, Cynthia, considering you'll be bearing the brunt of it. The prevailing winds are south-westerly, which means most of the muck will collect in Malvern House. Still – ' he paused to glance from her to Peter – 'you sow a wind and you reap a whirlwind, eh?'

There was a short silence.

'Have you noticed how Liam's wrecks have survived intact?' asked Nora then, with assumed brightness. 'Is it a judgement, do you think?'

'Don't be ridiculous,' said Jeremy.

Sam gave another brief chortle. 'Is it ridiculous? You complained enough when there were only the cars to worry about. Now you've got a burnt-out cottage as well. I can't believe the O'Riordans were insured, so it'll be years before anything is done. If you're lucky, a developer will buy the land and build an estate of little boxes on your doorstep. If you're unlucky, Liam will put up a corrugated-iron shack and live in that. And do you know, Jeremy, I hope he does! Personal revenge is so much sweeter than anything the law can offer.'

'What's that supposed to mean?'

'You'd have been wiser to call the fire brigade earlier,' said the old doctor bluntly. 'Nero may have fiddled while Rome burned, but it didn't do his reputation any good.'

Another silence.

'What are you implying?' demanded Cynthia aggressively. 'That Jeremy could somehow have prevented the fire?'

Jeremy Jardine folded his arms. 'I'll sue you for slander if you *are*, Sam.'

'It won't be just me. Half the village is wondering why Nora and I smelt burning before you did, and why Cynthia and Peter took themselves off to Salisbury on a Monday evening for the first time in living memory.'

'Coincidence,' grunted Peter Haversley. 'Pure coincidence.'

'Well, I pray for all your sakes you're telling the truth,' murmured Sam, wiping a weary hand across his ash-grimed face, 'because the police aren't the only ones who'll be asking questions. The Lavenhams certainly won't stay quiet.'

'I hope you're not suggesting that one of us set fire to that beastly little place,' said Cynthia crossly. 'Honestly, Sam, I wonder about you sometimes.'

He shook his head sadly, wishing he could dislike her as comprehensively as Siobhan Lavenham did. 'No, Cynthia, I'm suggesting you knew it was going to happen, and even incited the local youths to do it. You can argue that you wanted revenge for Lavinia and Dorothy's deaths, but aiding and abetting any crime is a prosecutable offence and – ' he sighed – 'you'll get no sympathy from me if you go to prison for it.'

Behind them, in the hall of Malvern House, the telephone began to ring . . .

*Wednesday, 10 February 1999*

Siobhan had put an opened envelope on the desk in front of the detective inspector. 'Even if Patrick is the murderer and even if Bridey knows he is, it doesn't excuse this kind of thing,' she said. 'I can't prove it came from Cynthia Haversley, but I'm a hundred per cent certain it did. She's busting a gut to make life so unpleasant for Liam and Bridey that they'll leave of their own accord.'

The inspector frowned as he removed a folded piece of paper and read the letters pasted onto it.

Hanging is too good
for the likes of you
Burn in hell

'Who was it sent to?' he asked.

'Bridey.'

'Why did she give it to you and not to the police?'

'Because she knew I was coming here today and asked me to bring it with me. It was posted through her letterbox sometime the night before last.'

('They'll take more notice of you than they ever take of me,' the old woman had said, pressing the envelope urgently into Siobhan's hands. 'Make them understand we're in danger before it's too late.')

He turned the envelope over. 'Why do you think it came from Mrs Haversley?'

Feminine intuition, thought Siobhan wryly. 'Because the letters that make up "hell" have been cut from a *Daily Telegraph* banner imprint. It's the only broad sheet newspaper that has an "h", an "e", and two "l"s in its title, and Cynthia takes the *Telegraph* every day.'

'Along with how many other people in Sower-bridge?'

She smiled slightly. 'Quite a few, but no one else has Cynthia Haversley's poisonous frame of mind. She loves stirring. The more she can work people up, the happier she is. It gives her a sense of importance to have everyone dancing to her tune.'

'You don't like her.' It was a statement rather than a question.

'No.'

'Neither do I,' admitted the inspector, 'but it doesn't make her guilty, Mrs Lavenham. Liam and/or Bridey could have acquired a *Telegraph* just as easily and sent this letter to themselves.'

'That's what Bridey told me you'd say.'

'Because it's the truth?' he suggested mildly. 'Mrs Haversley's a fat, clumsy woman with fingers like sausages, and if she'd been wearing gloves the whole exercise would have been impossible. This – ' he touched the letter – 'is too neat. There's not a letter out of place.'

'Peter then.'

'Peter Haversley's an alcoholic. His hands shake.'

'Jeremy Jardine?'

'I doubt it. Poison-pen letters are usually written by women. I'm sorry, Mrs Lavenham, but I can guarantee the only fingerprints I will find on this – other than yours and mine, of course – are Bridey O'Riordan's. Not because the person who did it wore gloves, but because Bridey did it herself.'

## Tuesday, 9 March 1999, 1.10 a.m.

Dr Bentley clicked his tongue in concern as he glanced past Cynthia to her husband. Peter was walking unsteadily towards them after answering the telephone, his face leeched of colour in the lights of the fire engines. 'You should be in bed, man. We should all be in bed. We're too old for this sort of excitement.'

Peter Haversley ignored him. 'That was Siobhan,' he said jerkily. 'She wants me to tell the police that Rosheen is missing. She said Liam called the farm from Kilkenny Cottage at eight thirty this evening, and she's worried he and Rosheen were in there when the fire started.'

'They can't have been,' said Jeremy.

'How do you know?'

'We watched Liam and Bridey leave for Winchester this morning.'

'What if Liam came back to protect his house? What if he phoned Rosheen and asked her to join him?'

'Oh, for God's sake, Peter!' snapped Cynthia. 'It's just Siobhan trying to make trouble again. You know what she's like.'

'I don't think so. She sounded very distressed.'

He looked around for a policeman. 'I'd better report it.'

But his wife gripped his arm to hold him back. 'No,' she said viciously. 'Let Siobhan do her own dirty work. If she wants to employ a slut to look after her children then it's her responsibility to keep tabs on her, not ours.'

There was a moment of stillness while Peter searched her face in appalled recognition that he was looking at a stranger, then he drew back his hand and slapped her across her face. 'Whatever depths you may have sunk to,' he said, 'I am *not* a murderer . . .'

**LATE NEWS Daily Telegraph**
*Tuesday, 9 March, a.m.*

## Irish Family Burnt Out by Vigilantes

The family home of Patrick O'Riordan, currently on trial for the murder of Lavinia Fanshaw and Dorothy Jenkins, was burnt to the ground last night in what police suspect was a deliberate act of arson. Concern has been expressed over the whereabouts of O'Riordan's elderly parents, and some reports suggest bodies were recovered from the gutted kitchen. Police are refusing to confirm or deny the rumours. Suspicion has fallen on local vigilante groups who have been conducting a 'hate' campaign against the O'Riordan family. In face of criticism, Hampshire police have restated their policy of zero tolerance towards anyone who decides to take the law into his own hands. 'We will not hesitate to prosecute,' said a spokesman. 'Vigilantes should understand that arson is a very serious offence.'

# Six

When Siobhan heard a car pull into the driveway at six a.m. she prayed briefly, but with little hope, that someone had found Rosheen and brought her home. Hollow-eyed from lack of sleep, she opened her front door and stared at the two policemen on her doorstep. They looked like ghosts in the grey dawn light. Harbingers of doom, she thought, reading their troubled expressions. She recognized one of them as the detective inspector and the other as the young constable who had flagged her down the previous night. 'You'd better come in,' she said, pulling the door wide.

'Thank you.'

She led the way into the kitchen and dropped onto the cushion in front of the Aga again, cradling Patch in her arms. 'This is Bridey's dog,' she told them, stroking his muzzle. 'She adores him. *He* adores her. The trouble is he's a hopeless guard dog. He's like Bridey – ' tears of exhaustion sprang into her eyes –

'not overly bright – not overly brave – but as kind as kind can be.'

The two policemen stood awkwardly in front of her, unsure where to sit or what to say.

'You look terrible,' she said unevenly, 'so I presume you've come to tell me Rosheen is dead.'

'We don't know yet, Mrs Lavenham,' said the inspector, turning a chair to face her and lowering himself onto it. He gestured to the young constable to do the same. 'We found a body in the kitchen area, but it'll be some time before—' He paused, unsure how to continue.

'I'm afraid it was so badly burnt it was unrecognizable. We're waiting on the pathologist's report to give us an idea of the age and – ' he paused again – 'sex.'

'Oh, God!' she said dully. 'Then it must be Rosheen.'

'Why don't you think it's Bridey or Liam?'

'Because . . .' she broke off with a worried frown, 'I assumed the phone call was a hoax to frighten Rosheen. Oh, my God! Aren't they in Winchester?'

He looked troubled. 'They were escorted to a safe house at the end of yesterday's proceedings but it appears they left again shortly afterwards. There was no one to monitor them, you see. They had a direct line through to the local police station and we sent out regular patrols during the night. We were worried about trouble coming from outside, not that they might decide to return to Kilkenny Cottage without telling us.' He rubbed a hand around his jaw. 'There are recent tyre marks up at the manor. We think Liam may have parked his Ford there in order to push Bridey across the lawn and through the gate onto the footpath beside Kilkenny Cottage.'

She shook her head in bewilderment. 'Then why didn't you find three bodies?'

'Because the car isn't there now, Mrs Lavenham, and whoever died in Kilkenny Cottage probably died at the hands of Liam O'Riordan.'

## Wednesday, 10 February 1999

She had stood up at the end of her interview with the inspector. 'Do you know what I hate most about the English?' she said.

He shook his head.

'It never occurs to you, you might be wrong.' She placed her palm on the poison-pen letter on his desk. 'But you're wrong about this. Bridey cares about my opinion – she cares about *me* – not just as a fellow Irishwoman but as the employer of her niece. She'd never do anything to jeopardize Rosheen's position in our house because Rosheen and I are her only life-line in Sowerbridge. We shop for her, we do our best to protect her, and we welcome her to the farm when things get difficult. Under no circumstances *whatso-ever* would Bridey use me to pass on falsified evidence because she'd be too afraid I'd wash my hands of her and then persuade Rosheen to do the same.'

'It may be true, Mrs Lavenham, but it's not an argument you could ever use in court.'

'I'm not interested in legal argument, Inspector, I'm only interested in persuading you that there is a terror campaign being waged against the O'Riordans in Sowerbridge and that their lives are in danger.' She watched him shake his head. 'You haven't listened to a word I've said, have you? You just think I'm taking Bridey's side because I'm Irish.'

'Aren't you?'

No.' She straightened with a sigh. 'Moral support is alien to Irish culture, Inspector. We only really enjoy fighting with each other. I thought every Englishman knew *that* . . .'

### Tuesday, 9 March 1999, noon

The news that Patrick O'Riordan's trial had been adjourned while police investigated the disappearance of his parents and his cousin was broadcast across the networks at noon, but Siobhan switched off the radio before the names could register with her two young sons.

They had sat wide-eyed all morning watching a procession of policemen traipse to and from Rosheen's bedroom in search of anything that might give them a lead to where she had gone. Most poignantly, as far as Siobhan was concerned, they had carefully removed the girl's hairbrush, some used tissues from her waste-paper basket and a small pile of dirty washing in order to provide the pathologist with comparative DNA samples.

She had explained to the boys that Rosheen hadn't been in the house when she got back the previous night, and because she was worried about it she had asked the police to help find her.

'She went to Auntie Bridey's,' said six-year-old James.

'How do you know, darling?'

'Because Uncle Liam phoned and said Auntie Bridey wasn't feeling very well.'

'Did Rosheen tell you that?'

He nodded. 'She said she wouldn't be long but that I had to go to sleep. So I did.'

She dropped a kiss on the top of his head. 'Good boy.'

He and Oliver were drawing pictures at the kitchen table, and James suddenly dragged his pencil to and fro across the page to obliterate what he'd been doing. 'Is it because Uncle Patrick killed that lady?' he asked her.

Siobhan searched his face for a moment. *The rules had been very clear . . . Whatever else you do, Rosheen, please do not tell the children what Patrick has been accused of . . .* 'I didn't know you knew about that,' she said lightly.

'Everyone knows,' he told her solemnly. 'Uncle Patrick's a monster and ought to be strung up.'

'Goodness!' she exclaimed, forcing a smile to her lips. 'Who said that?'

'Kevin.'

Anger tightened like knots in her chest. *Ian had laid it on the line following the incident in the barn . . . You may see Kevin in your spare time, Rosheen, but not when you're in charge of the children . . .* 'Kevin Wyllie? Rosheen's friend?' She squatted down beside him, smoothing a lock of hair from his forehead. 'Does he come here a lot?'

'Rosheen said we weren't to tell.'

'I don't think she meant you musn't tell me, darling.'

James wrapped his thin little arms round her neck and pressed his cheek against hers. 'I think she did, Mummy. She said Kevin would rip her head off if we told you and Daddy anything.'

## Tuesday, 9 March 1999, later

'I can't believe I let this happen,' she told the inspector, pacing up and down her drawing room in a frenzy of movement. 'I should have listened to Ian. He said Kevin was no good the minute he saw him.'

'Calm down, Mrs Lavenham,' he said quietly. 'I imagine your children can hear every word you're saying.'

'But why didn't Rosheen tell me Kevin was threatening her? God knows, she should have known she could trust me. I've bent over backwards to help her and her family.'

'Perhaps that's the problem,' he suggested. 'Perhaps she was worried about laying any more burdens on your shoulders.'

'But she was responsible for my *children*, for God's sake! I can't believe she'd keep quiet while some low-grade neanderthal was terrorizing her.'

The inspector watched her for a moment, wondering how much to tell her. 'Kevin Wyllie is also missing,' he said abruptly. 'We're collecting DNA samples from his bedroom because we think the body at Kilkenny Cottage is his.'

Siobhan stared at him in bewilderment. 'I don't understand.'

He gave a hollow laugh. 'The one thing the pathologist *can* be certain about, Mrs Lavenham, is that the body was upright when it died.'

'I still don't understand.'

He looked ill, she thought, as he ran his tongue across dry lips. 'We're working on the theory that Liam, Bridey and Rosheen appointed themselves judge, jury and hangman before setting fire to Kilkenny Cottage in order to destroy the evidence.'

**Daily Telegraph – *Wednesday, 10 March, a.m.***

## Couple Arrested

Two people, believed to be the parents of Patrick O'Riordan, whose trial at Winchester Crown Court was adjourned two days ago, were arrested on suspicion of murder in Liverpool yesterday as they attempted to board a ferry to Ireland. There is still no clue to the whereabouts of their niece Rosheen, whose family lives in County Donegal. Hampshire police have admitted that the Irish Garda have been assisting them in their search for the missing family. Suspicion remains that the body found in Kilkenny Cottage was that of Sowerbridge resident Kevin Wyllie, 28, although police refuse to confirm or deny the story.

*Thursday, 11 March 1999, 4.00 a.m.*

Siobhan had lain awake for hours, listening to the clock on the bedside table tick away the seconds. She heard Ian come in at two o'clock and tiptoe into the spare room, but she didn't call out to tell him she was awake. There would be time enough to say sorry tomorrow. Sorry for dragging him home early . . . sorry for saying Lavenham Interiors could go down the drain for all she cared . . . sorry for getting everything so wrong . . . sorry for blaming the English for the sins of the Irish . . .

Grief squeezed her heart every time she thought about Rosheen. But it was a complicated grief that carried shame and guilt in equal proportions because she couldn't rid herself of responsibility for what the girl had done. 'I thought she was keen on Kevin,' she told the inspector that afternoon. 'Ian never understood the attaction, but I did.'

'Why?' he asked with a hint of cynicism. 'Because it was a suitable match? Because Kevin was the same class as she was?'

'It wasn't a question of class,' she protested.

'Wasn't it? In some ways you're more of a snob than the English, Mrs Lavenham. You forced Rosheen to acknowledge her relationship with Liam and Bridey because *you* acknowledged them,' he told her brutally, 'but it really ought to have occurred to you that a bright girl like her would have higher ambitions than to be known as the niece of Irish gypsies.'

'Then why bother with Kevin at all? Wasn't he just as bad?'

The inspector shrugged. 'What choice did she have? How many unattached men are there in Sowerbridge? And you had to believe she was with someone, Mrs Lavenham, otherwise you'd have started asking awkward questions. Still – ' he paused – 'I doubt the poor lad had any idea just how much she loathed him.'

'No one did,' said Siobhan sadly. 'Everyone thought she was besotted with him after the incident in the barn.'

'She was playing a long game,' he said slowly, 'and she was very good at it. You never doubted she was fond of her aunt and uncle.'

'I believed what she told me.'

He smiled slightly. 'And you were determined that everyone else should believe it as well.'

Siobhan looked at him with stricken eyes. 'Oh God! Does that make it my fault?'

'No,' he murmured. 'Mine. I didn't take you seriously when you said the Irish only really enjoy fighting each other.'

### Thursday, 11 March 1999, 3.00 p.m.

Cynthia Haversley opened her front door a crack. 'Oh, it's you,' she said with surprising warmth. 'I thought it was another of those beastly journalists.'

Well, well! How quickly times change, thought Siobhan ruefully as she stepped inside. Not so long ago Cynthia had been inviting those same 'beastly' journalists into Malvern House for cups of tea while she regaled them with stories about the O'Riordans' iniquities. Siobhan nodded to Peter, who was standing in the doorway to the drawing room. 'How are you both?'

It was three days since she had seen them; and she was surprised by how much they had aged. Peter, in particular, looked haggard and grey, and she assumed he must have been hitting the bottle harder than usual. He made a rocking motion with his hand. 'Not too good. Rather ashamed about the way we've all been behaving, if I'm honest.'

Cynthia opened her mouth to say something, but clearly thought better of it. 'Where are the boys?' she asked instead.

'Nora's looking after them for me.'

'You should have brought them with you. I wouldn't have minded.'

Siobhan shook her head. 'I didn't want them to hear what I'm going to say to you, Cynthia.'

The woman bridled immediately. 'You can't blame—'

'Enough!' snapped Peter, cutting her short and stepping to one side. 'Come into the drawing room, Siobhan. How's Ian bearing up? We saw he'd come home.'

She walked across to the window, from where she could see the remains of Kilkenny Cottage. 'Tired,' she answered. 'He didn't get back till early this morning and he had to leave again at crack of dawn for the office. We've got three contracts on the go and they're all going pear-shaped because neither of us has been there.'

'It can't be easy for you.'

'No,' she said slowly, 'it's not. Ian was supposed to stay in Italy till Friday, but as things are . . .' She paused. 'Neither of us can be in two places at once, unfortunately.' She turned to look at them. 'And I can't leave the children.'

'I'm sorry,' said Peter.

She gave a small laugh. 'There's no need to be. I do rather like them, you know, so it's no hardship having to stay at home. I just wish it hadn't had to happen this way.' She folded her arms and studied Cynthia seriously. 'James told me an interesting story yesterday,' she said. 'I assume it's true because he's a truthful child, but I thought I'd check it with you anyway. In view of everything that's happened, I'm hesitant to accept anyone's word on anything. Did you go down to the farm one day and find James and Oliver alone?'

'I saw Rosheen leave,' she said, 'but I knew no one was there to look after them because I'd been – well – watching the drive that morning.' She puffed out her chest in self-defence. 'I told you she was deceitful and lazy but you wouldn't listen to me.'

'Because you never told me why,' said Siobhan mildly.

'I assumed you knew and that it didn't bother you. Ian made no secret of how angry he was when you came home one night and found her with Kevin in the barn, but you just said he was overreacting.' Cynthia considered the wisdom of straight speaking, decided it was necessary, and took a deep breath. 'If I'm honest, Siobhan, you even seemed to find it rather amusing. I never understood why. Personally, I'd have sacked her on the spot and looked for someone more respectable.'

Siobhan shook her head. 'I thought it was a one-off. I didn't realize she'd been making a habit of it.'

'She was too interested in sex not to, my dear. I've never seen anyone so shameless. More often than not, she'd leave your boys with Bridey if it meant she could have a couple of hours with Kevin Wyllie. Many's the time I watched her sneak them into Kilkenny Cottage only to sauce out again five minutes later on her own. And then she'd drive off in your Range Rover, bold as brass, with that unpleasant young man beside her.

I did wonder if you knew what your car was being used for.'

'You should have told me.'

Cynthia shook her head. 'You wouldn't have listened.'

'In fact, Cynthia tried several times to broach the subject,' said Peter gently, 'but on each occasion you shot her down in flames and all but accused her of being an anti-Irish bigot.'

'I never had much choice,' murmured Siobhan, without hostility. 'Could you not have divorced Rosheen from Liam, Bridey and Patrick, Cynthia? Why did every conversation about my nanny have to begin with a diatribe against her relatives?'

There was a short, uncomfortable silence.

Siobhan sighed. 'What I really don't understand is why you should have thought I was the kind of mother who wouldn't care if her children were being neglected.'

Cynthia looked embarrassed. 'I didn't, not really. I just thought you were – well, rather more relaxed than most.'

'Because I'm Irish and not English?'

Peter tut-tutted in concern. 'It wasn't like that,' he said. 'Hang it all, Siobhan, we didn't know what Rosheen's instructions were. To be honest, we thought you were encouraging her to make use of Bridey in order to give the poor old thing a sense of purpose. We didn't applaud your strategy – as a matter of fact, it seemed like a mad idea to us—'

He broke off with a guilty expression. 'As Cynthia kept saying, there's no way she'd have left two boisterous children in the care of a disabled woman and a drunken man, but we thought you were trying to demonstrate solidarity with them. If I trust the O'Riordans with my children, then so should the rest of you . . . that sort of thing.'

Siobhan turned back to the window and the blackened heap that had been Kilkenny Cottage. *For want of a nail the shoe was lost . . . for want of a shoe the horse was lost . . . for want of mutual understanding lives were lost . . .* 'Couldn't you have told me about the time you went to the farm and found James and Oliver on their own?' she murmured, her breath misting the glass.

'I did,' said Cynthia.

'When?'

'The day after I found them. I stopped you and Ian at the end of the drive as you were setting off for work and told you your children were too young to be left alone. I must say I thought your attitude was extraordinarily casual but – well – ' she shrugged – 'I'd rather come to expect that.'

Siobhan remembered the incident well. Cynthia had stood in the drive, barring their way, and had then thrust her indignant red face through Ian's open window and lectured them on the foolishness of employing a girl with loose morals. 'We both assumed you were talking about the night she took Kevin into the barn. Ian said afterwards that he wished he'd never mentioned it because you were using it as a stick to beat us.'

Cynthia frowned. 'Didn't James and Oliver tell you about it? I sat with them for nearly two hours, in all conscience, and gave Rosheen a piece of my mind when she finally came back.'

'They were too frightened. Kevin beat them about the head because they'd opened the door to you and said if I ever asked them if Mrs Haversley had come to the house they were to say no.'

Cynthia lowered herself carefully onto a chair. 'I had no idea,' she said in an appalled tone of voice. 'No wonder you took it so calmly.'

'Mm.' Siobhan glanced from the seated woman to her husband. 'We seem to have got our wires crossed all along the line, and I feel very badly about it now. I keep thinking that if I hadn't been so quick to condemn you all, *no one* would have died.'

Peter shook his head. 'We all feel the same way. Even Sam and Nora Bentley. They're saying that if they'd backed your judgement of Liam and Bridey instead of sitting on the fence—' He broke off on a sigh. 'I can't understand why we allowed it to get so out of hand. We're not unkind people. A little misguided . . . rather too easily prejudiced perhaps . . . but not *unkind*.'

Siobhan thought of Jeremy Jardine. Was Peter including Lavinia's grandson in this general absolution, she wondered.

# Seven

*Friday, 12 March 1999, 9.00 a.m.*

'Can I get you a cup of tea, Bridey?' asked the inspector as he came into the interview room.

The old woman's eyes twinkled mischievously. 'I'd rather have a Guinness.'

He laughed as he pulled out a chair. 'You and Liam both. He says it's the first time he's been on the wagon since his last stretch in prison nearly twenty years ago.' He studied her for a moment. 'Any regrets?'

'Only the one,' she said. 'That we didn't kill Mr Jardine as well.'

'No regrets about killing Rosheen?'

'Why would I have?' she asked him. 'I'd crush a snake as easily. She taunted us with how clever she'd been to kill two harmless old ladies and then have my poor Patrick take the blame. And all for the sake of marrying a rich man. I should have recognized her as the devil the first day I saw her.'

'How did you kill her?'

'She was a foolish girl. She thought that because I'm in a wheelchair she had nothing to fear from me, when, of course, every bit of strength I have is in my arms. It was Liam she was afraid of, but she should have remembered that Liam hasn't been able to hurt a fly these fifteen years.' She smiled as she released the arm of her wheelchair and held it up. The two metal prongs that located it in the chair's framework protruded from each end. 'I can only shift myself to a bed or a chair when this is removed, and it's been lifted out that many times the ends are like razors. Perhaps I'd not have brought it down on her wicked head if she hadn't laughed and called us illiterate Irish trash. Then again, perhaps I would. To be sure, I was angry enough.'

'Why weren't you angry with Kevin?' he asked curiously. 'He says he was only there that night because he'd been paid to set fire to your house. Why didn't you kill him, too? He's making no bones about the fact that he and his friends have been terrorizing you for months.'

'Do you think we didn't know that? Why would we go back to Kilkenny Cottage in secret if it wasn't to catch him and his friends red-handed and make you coppers sit up and take notice of the fearful things they've been doing to us these many months? As Liam said, fight fire with fire. Mind, that's not to say we wanted to kill them – give them a shock, maybe.'

'But only Kevin turned up?'

She nodded. 'Poor greedy creature that he is.

Would he share good money with his friends when a single match would do the business? He came creeping in with his petrol can and I've never seen a lad so frightened as when Liam slipped the noose about his throat and called to me to switch on the light. We'd strung it from the beams and the lad was caught like a fly on a web. Did we tell you he wet himself?'

'No.'

'Well, he did. Pissed all over the floor in terror.'

'He's got an inch-wide rope burn round his neck, Bridey. Liam must have pulled the noose pretty tight for that, so perhaps Kevin thought you were going to hang him?'

'Liam hasn't the strength to pull anything tight,' she said matter-of-factly, slotting the chair arm back into its frame. 'Not these fifteen years.'

'So you keep saying,' murmured the inspector.

'I expect Kevin will tell you he slipped and did it himself. He was that frightened he could hardly keep his feet, but at least it meant we knew he was telling the truth. He could have named anybody . . . Mrs Haversley . . . Mr Jardine . . . but instead he told us it was our niece who had promised him a hundred quid if he'd burn Kilkenny Cottage down and get us out of her hair for good.'

'Did he also say she had been orchestrating the campaign against you?'

'Oh, yes,' she murmured, staring past him as her mind replayed the scene in her head. ' "She calls you thieving Irish trash," he said, "and hates you for your cheap, common ways and your poverty. She wants rid of you from Sowerbridge because people will never treat her right until you're gone." ' She smiled slightly. 'So I told him I didn't blame her, that it can't have been easy having her cousin arrested for murder and her aunt and uncle treated like lepers – ' she paused to stare at her hands – 'and he said Patrick's arrest had nothing to do with it.'

'Did he explain what he meant?'

'That she'd hated us from the first day she met us.' She shook her head. 'Though, to be sure, I don't know what we did to make her think so badly of us.'

'You lied to your family, Bridey. We've spoken to her brother. According to him, her mother filled her head with stories about how rich you and Liam were and how you'd sold your business in London to retire to a beautiful cottage in a beautiful part of England. I think the reality must have been a terrible disappointment to her. According to her brother, she came over from Ireland with dreams of meeting a wealthy man and marrying him.'

'She was wicked through and through, Inspector, and I'll not take any of her fault on me. I was honest with her from the beginning. We are as you see us, I said, because God saw fit to punish us for Liam and Patrick's wrongdoing, but you'll never be embarrassed by it because no one knows. We may not be as rich as you hoped, but we're loving, and there'll always be a home for you here if the job doesn't work out with Mrs Lavenham.'

'Now Mrs Lavenham's blaming herself, Bridey. She says if she'd spent less time at the office and more with Rosheen and the children, no one would have died.'

Distress creased Bridey's forehead. 'It's always the same when people abandon their religion. Without God in their lives, they quickly lose sight of the devil. Yet for you and me, Inspector, the devil exists in the hearts of the wicked. Mrs Lavenham needs reminding that it was Rosheen who betrayed this family . . . and only Rosheen.'

'Because you gave her the means when you told her about Patrick's conviction.'

The old woman's mouth thinned into a narrow line. 'And she used it against him. Can you believe that I never once questioned why those poor old ladies were killed with Patrick's hammer? Would you not think – knowing my boy was innocent – that I'd have put two and two together and said, there's no such thing as coincidence?'

'She was clever,' said the inspector. 'She made everyone believe she was only interested in Kevin Wyllie, and Kevin Wyllie had no reason on earth to murder Mrs Fanshaw.'

'I have it in my heart to feel sorry for the poor lad now,' said Bridey with a small laugh, 'never mind he terrorized us for months. Rosheen showed her colours soon enough when she came down after Liam's phone call to find Kevin trussed up like a chicken on the floor. That's when I saw the cunning in her eyes and realized for the first time what a schemer she was. She tried to pretend Kevin was lying, but when she saw we didn't believe her, she snatched the petrol can from the table. "I'll make you burn in hell, you stupid, incompetent bastard," she told him. "You've served your purpose, made everyone think I was interested in you when you're so far beneath me I wouldn't have wasted a second glance on you if I hadn't had to." Then she came towards me, unscrewing the lid of the petrol can as she did so and slopping it over my skirt. Bold as brass she was with her lighter in her hand, telling Liam she'd set fire to me if he tried to stop her phoning her fancy man to come and help her.' Her eyes hardened at the memory. 'She couldn't keep quiet, of course. Perhaps people can't when they believe in their own cleverness. She told us how gullible we were . . . what excitement she'd had battering two old ladies to death . . . how besotted Mr Jardine was with her . . . how easy it had been to cast suspicion on a moron like Patrick . . . And when Mr Jardine never answered because he was hiding in his cellar, she turned on me in a fury and thrust the lighter against my skirt, saying she'd burn us all anyway. Kevin will get the blame, she said, even though he'll be dead. Half the village knows he's been sent down here to do the business.'

'And that's when you hit her?'

Bridey nodded. 'I certainly wasn't going to wait for her to strike the flint, now was I?'

'And Kevin witnessed all this?'

'He did indeed, and will say so at my trial if you decide to prosecute me.'

The inspector smiled slightly. 'So who set the house on fire, Bridey?'

'To be sure, it was Rosheen who did it. The petrol spilled all over the floor as she fell and the lighter sparked as it hit the quarry tiles.' A flicker of amusement crossed her old face as she looked at him. 'Ask young Kevin if you don't believe me.'

'I already have. He agrees with you. The only trouble is, he breaks out in a muck sweat every time the question's put to him.'

'And why wouldn't he? It was a terrible experience for all of us.'

'So why didn't you go up in flames, Bridey? You said your skirt was saturated with petrol.'

'Ah, well, do you not think that was God's doing?' She crossed herself. 'Of course, it may have had something to do with the fact that Kevin had managed to free himself and was able to push me to the door while Liam smothered the flames with his coat, but for myself I count it a miracle.'

'You're lying through your teeth, Bridey. We think Liam started the fire on purpose in order to hide something.'

The old woman gave a cackle of laughter. 'Now why would you think that, Inspector? What could two poor cripples have done that they didn't want the police to know about?' Her eyes narrowed. 'Never mind a witch had tried to rob them of their only son?'

*Friday, 12 March 1999, 2.00 p.m.*

'Did you find out?' Siobhan asked the inspector.

He shrugged. 'We think Kevin had to watch a ritual burning and is too terrified to admit to it because he's the one who took the petrol there in the first place.' He watched a look of disbelief cross Siobhan's face. 'Bridey called her a witch,' he reminded her.

Siobhan shook her head. 'And you think that's the evidence Liam wanted to destroy?'

'Yes.'

She gave an unexpected laugh. 'You must think the Irish are very backward, Inspector. Didn't ritual burnings go out with the Middle Ages?' She paused, unable to control her amusement. 'Are you going to charge them with it? The press will love it if you do. I can just imagine the headlines when the case comes to trial.'

'No,' he said, watching her. 'Kevin's sticking to the story Liam and Bridey taught him, and the pathologist's suggestion that Rosheen was upright when she died looks too damn flakey to take into court. At the moment, we're accepting a plea of self-defence and accidental arson.' He paused. 'Unless you know differently, Mrs Lavenham.'

Her expression was unreadable. 'All I know,' she

told him, 'is that Bridey could no more have burnt her niece as a witch than she could get up out of her wheelchair and walk. But don't go by what I say, Inspector. I've been wrong about everything else.'

'Mm. Well, you're right. Their defence against murder rests entirely on their disabilities.'

Siobhan seemed to lose interest and fell into a thoughtful silence which the inspector was loath to break. 'Was it Rosheen who told you Patrick had stolen Lavinia's jewellery?' she demanded abruptly.

'Why do you ask?'

'Because I've never understood why you suddenly concentrated all your efforts on him.'

'We found his fingerprints at the manor.'

'Along with mine and most of Sowerbridge's.'

'But yours aren't on file, Mrs Lavenham, and you don't have a criminal record.'

'Neither should Patrick, Inspector, not if it's fifteen years since he committed a crime. The English have a strong sense of justice, and that means his slate should have been wiped clean after seven years. Someone – ' she studied him curiously – 'must have pointed the finger at him. I've never been able to work out who it was, but perhaps it was you? Did you base your whole case against him on privileged knowledge that you acquired fifteen years ago in London? If so, you're a shit.'

He was irritated enough to defend himself. 'He boasted to Rosheen about how he'd got the better of a senile old woman and showed her Mrs Fanshaw's jewellery to prove it. She said he was full of himself, talked about how both old women were so ga-ga they'd given him the run of the house in return for doing some small maintenance jobs. She didn't say Patrick had murdered them – she was too clever for that – but when we questioned Patrick and he denied ever being in the Manor House or knowing anything about any stolen jewellery, we decided to search Kilkenny Cottage and came up trumps.'

'Which is what Rosheen wanted.'

'We know that now, Mrs Lavenham, and if Patrick had been straight with us from the beginning, it might have been different then. But, unfortunately, he wasn't. His difficulty was he had the old lady's rings in his possession as well as the costume jewellery that Miss Jenkins gave him. He knew perfectly well he'd been palmed off with worthless glass, so he hopped upstairs when Miss Jenkins's back was turned and helped himself to something more valuable. He claims Mrs Fanshaw was asleep so he just slipped the rings off her fingers and tiptoed out again.'

'Did Bridey and Rosheen know he'd taken the rings?'

'Yes, but he told them they were glass replicas which had been in the box with the rest of the bits and pieces. Rosheen knew differently, of course – she and Jardine understood Patrick's psychology well enough to know he'd steal something valuable the minute his earnings were denied – but Bridey believed him.'

She nodded. 'Has Jeremy admitted his part in it?'

'Not yet,' murmured the inspector dryly, 'but he will. He's a man without scruples. He recognized a fellow traveller in Rosheen, seduced her with promises of marriage, then persuaded her to kill his grandmother and her nurse so that he could inherit. Rosheen didn't need an alibi – she was never even questioned about where she was that night because you all assumed she was with Kevin.'

'On the principle that shagging Kevin was the only thing that interested her,' agreed Siobhan. 'She *was* clever, you know. No one suspected for a minute that she was having an affair with Jeremy. Cynthia Haversley thought she was a common little tart. Ian thought Kevin was taking advantage of her. *I* thought she was having a good time.'

'She was. She had her future mapped out as Lady of the Manor once Patrick was convicted and Jardine inherited the damn place. Apparently, her one ambition in life was to lord it over Liam and Bridey. If you're interested, Mrs Haversley is surprisingly sympathetic towards her.' He lifted a cynical eyebrow. 'She says she recognizes how easy it must have been for a degenerate like Jardine to manipulate an unsophisticated country girl when he had no trouble persuading *sophisticated* – ' he drew quote marks in the air – 'types like her and Mr Haversley to believe whatever he told them.'

Siobhan smiled. 'I'm growing quite fond of her in a funny sort of way. It's like fighting your way through a blackened baked potato. The outside's revolting but the inside's delicious and rather soft.' Her eyes strayed towards the window, searching for some distant horizon. 'The odd thing is, Nora Bentley told me on Monday that it was a pity I'd never seen the kind side of Cynthia . . . and I had the bloody nerve to say I didn't want to. God, how I wish—' She broke off abruptly, unwilling to reveal too much of the anguish that still churned inside her. 'Why did Liam and Bridey take Kevin with them?' she asked next.

'According to him, they all panicked. *He* was scared he'd get the blame for burning the house down with Rosheen in it if he stayed behind, and *they* were scared the police would think they'd done it on purpose to prejudice Patrick's trial. He claims he left them when they got to Liverpool because he has a friend up there he hadn't seen for ages.'

'And according to you?'

'We don't think he had any choice. We think Liam dragged him by the noose round his neck and only released him when they were sure he'd stick by the story they'd concocted.'

'Why were Liam and Bridey going to Ireland?'

'According to them, or according to us?'

'According to them.'

'Because they were frightened . . . because they knew it would take time for the truth to come out . . . because they had nowhere else to go . . . because everything they owned had been destroyed . . . because Ireland was home . . .'

'And according to you?'

'They guessed Kevin would start to talk as soon as he got over his fright, so they decided to run.'

She gave a low laugh. 'You can't have it both ways, Inspector. If they released him because they were sure he'd stick by the story, then they didn't need to run. And if they knew they could never be sure of him – as they most certainly should have done if they'd performed a ritual murder – he would have died with Rosheen.'

'Then what are they trying to hide?'

She was amazed he couldn't see it. 'Probably nothing,' she hedged. 'You're just in the habit of never believing anything they say.'

He gave a stubborn shake of his head. 'No, there *is* something. I've known them too long not to know when they're lying.'

He would go on until he found out, she thought. He was that kind of man. And when he did, his suspicion about Rosheen's death would immediately raise its ugly head again. Unless . . . 'The trouble with the O'Riordans,' she said, 'is that they can never see the wood for the trees. Patrick's just spent nine months on remand because he was more afraid of being charged with what he *had* done . . . theft . . . than what he *hadn't* done . . . murder. I suspect Liam and Bridey are doing the same – desperately trying to hide the crime they have committed, without realizing they're digging an even bigger hole for themselves for the one they haven't.'

'Go on.'

Siobhan's eyes twinkled as mischievously as Bridey's had done. 'Off the record?' she asked him. 'I won't say another word otherwise.'

'Can they be charged with it?'

'Oh, yes, but I doubt it'll trouble your conscience much if you don't report it.'

He was too curious not to give her the go-ahead. 'Off the record,' he agreed.

'All right, I think it goes something like this. Liam and Bridey have been living off the English taxpayer for fifteen years. They got disability benefit for his paralysed arm, disability benefit for her broken pelvis, and Patrick gets a care allowance for looking after both of them. They get mobility allowances, heating allowances and anything else you can think of.' She tipped her forefinger at him. 'But Kevin's built like a gorilla and prides himself on his physique, and Rosheen was as tall as I am. So how did a couple of elderly cripples manage to overpower both of them?'

'You tell me.'

'At a guess, Liam wielded his useless arm to hold them in a bear hug while Bridey leapt up out of her chair to tie them up. Bridey would call it a miracle cure. Social services would call it deliberate fraud. It depends how easily you think English doctors can be fooled by professional malingerers.'

He was visibly shocked. 'Are you saying Patrick never disabled either of them?'

Her rich laughter peeled round the room. 'He must have done at the time. You can't fake a shattered wrist and a broken pelvis, but I'm guessing Liam and Bridey probably prolonged their own agony in order to milk sympathy and money out of the system.' She canted her head to one side. 'Don't you find it interesting that they decided to move away from the doctors who'd been treating them in London to hide themselves in the wilds of Hampshire where the only person competent to sign their benefit forms is – er – medically speaking – well, past his sell-by date? You've met Sam Bentley. Do you seriously think it would ever occur to him to question whether two people who'd been registered disabled by a leading London hospital were ripping off the English taxpayer?'

'Jesus!' He shook his head. 'But why did they need to burn the house down? What would we have found that was so incriminating? Apart from Rosheen's body, of course.'

'Sets of fingerprints from Liam's right hand all over the door knobs?' Siobhan suggested. 'The marks of Bridey's shoes on the kitchen floor? However Rosheen died – whether in self-defence or not – they couldn't afford to report it because you'd have sealed off Kilkenny Cottage immediately while you tried to work out what happened.'

The inspector looked interested. 'And it wouldn't have taken us long to realize that neither of them is as disabled as they claim to be.'

'No.'

'And we'd have arrested them immediately on suspicion of murder.'

She nodded. 'Just as you did Patrick.'

He acknowledged the point with a grudging smile. 'Do you know all this for a fact, Mrs Lavenham?'

'No,' she replied. 'Just guessing. And I'm certainly not going to repeat it in court. It's irrelevant anyway. The evidence went up in flames.'

'Not if I get a doctor to certify they're as agile as I am.'

'That doesn't prove they were agile before the fire,' she pointed out. 'Bridey will find a specialist to quote psychosomatic paralysis at you, and Sam Bentley's never going to admit to being fooled by a couple of malingerers.' She chuckled. 'Neither will Cynthia Haversley, if it comes to that. She's been watching them out of her window for years, and she's never suspected a thing. In any case, Bridey's a great believer in miracles, and she's already told you it was God who rescued them from the inferno.'

'She must think I'm an absolute idiot.'

'Not you personally. Just your . . . er . . . kind.'

He frowned ominously. 'What's that supposed to mean?'

Siobhan studied him with amusement. 'The Irish have been getting the better of the English for centuries, Inspector.' She watched his eyes narrow in instinctive denial. 'And if the English weren't so blinded by their own self-importance,' she finished mischievously, 'they might have noticed.'

# The Devil's Feather

**The new novel by Minette Walters will
be published by Macmillan in October 2005**

*With private security firms supplying bodyguards in
every theatre of war, who will notice the emergence of
a sexual psychopath from the ranks of the mercenaries?*

When five women are brutally murdered in Sierra
Leone Reuters' correspondent, Connie Burns, ques-
tions the arrest of three rebel soldiers for the crimes.
No one listens.

With little to go on except her witnessing of a savage attack on a prostitute, Connie believes a foreigner
is responsible: a man who claims to have been in the
SAS and who works as a bodyguard for a Lebanese
diamond trader. She remembers him from Kinshasa,
when he was a mercenary for Laurent Kabila's regime,
and she suspects he uses the chaos of war to act out
sadistic fantasies against women.

Two years later in Iraq the consequences of
her second attempt to expose him are devastating.

Terrified, degraded and destroyed, she goes into hiding in England, where she strikes up a friendship with Jess Derbyshire, a loner whose reclusive nature has alienated her from the rest of the Dorset community where she lives. Seeing parallels between herself and Jess, Connie borrows from the other woman's strength and makes the hazardous decision to attempt a third unmasking of a serial killer – knowing he will come looking for her . . .

*An extract from this*
*powerful psychological thriller follows*

'The secret of happiness is freedom; the secret of freedom, courage'

– Thucydides (Greek historian, BC)

**Devil's Feather** – (derivation Turkish) – a woman who stirs a man's interest without realizing it; the unwitting cause of sexual arousal

>>> **Reuters**
>>> Wednesday, 15 May 2002, 16:17 GMT 17:17 UK
>>> Filed by Connie Burns, Freetown, Sierra Leone,
    West Africa

**Spate of Brutal Killings**

Four months after President Kabbah announced an end
to Sierra Leone's bloody civil war a spate of brutal
killings in Freetown threatens to undermine the fragile
peace. Police blame former rebel soldiers for the savage
murders. Attacked at intervals since peace was declared
in January, the five victims were found raped and
hacked to death in their own homes.

A government source said yesterday, 'The killing of
these women bears the trademark ferocity of the
rebels. Sierra Leone has just emerged from a decade of
savage conflict, and police believe a group of dissidents
is responsible. We call on everyone to put an end to
bloodshed.'

Detective Inspector Alan Collins of Manchester CID,
who is in Freetown as part of a British training force,
points to the serial nature of the murders. 'It's difficult
to say how many people are involved at this stage, but

121

the evidence suggests the crimes are linked. We are looking for a disturbed individual, or group, who acquired a taste for killing during the war. Rape and murder were commonplace, and violence against women doesn't stop just because peace is declared.'

>>> **Reuters**
>>> Tuesday, 4 June 2002, 13:06 GMT 14:06 UK
>>> Filed by Connie Burns, Freetown, Sierra Leone,
      West Africa

**Three Suspects Charged**

Three teenagers, formerly members of Foday Sankoh's
RUF child army, were charged yesterday with the
murders of five women. They were arrested after the
attempted abduction of Amie Jonah, 14. Ahmad
Gberebana, 19, Johnny Bunumbu, 19, and Katema
Momana, 18, were caught and detained by Miss
Jonah's family when the girl's screams alerted a
neighbour.

A police spokesman said the teenagers were badly
beaten before being handed over to the authorities.
'They caused great distress to Miss Jonah,' he said, 'and
her father and brothers were understandably angry.'
Fear has been rampant in Freetown since the gruesome
discoveries of five murdered women. All were raped
and disfigured by machete wounds.

In two cases identification was impossible. 'They may
never be named,' said Detective Inspector Alan Collins
of Manchester Police, who is advising the enquiry team.

'The civil war saw nearly half of this country's
4.5 million population displaced and we've no idea
which area these women came from.'

He confirmed that a request for a British pathologist
to provide expert assistance has been withdrawn.
'I understand that Gberebana, Bunumbu and Momana
have provided police with full details of the murders.
Investigators are satisfied they have the right men in
custody.'

The three teenagers were given medical treatment
before being transferred to Pademba Road prison to
await trial.

# One

I don't know if that story was picked up in the West. I believe some interest was shown in South Africa, but only because rape and murder had been high on the agenda there for some time. I was transferred to Asia shortly afterwards, so I never learnt the outcome of the trial. I assumed the teenagers were convicted because they were charged after full confessions, and justice, like everything else in Sierra Leone, was subject to economic restrictions. Even if the court went to the expense of appointing a public defence lawyer, confessions of guilt, with full and graphic details of how each victim was murdered, would attract a summary sentence.

I know Alan Collins was troubled by the indictments, but there was little he could do about it when his request for an experienced pathologist was refused. He was in a difficult position – more an observer than an adviser – with less than two weeks of his secondment left at the time of Amie Jonah's abduction, and the youths' descriptions of their crimes effectively sealed their fate. Nevertheless, Alan remained sceptical about the confessions.

'They were in no fit state to be questioned,' he told me. 'Amie's family had reduced them to pulp. They'd have said anything the police wanted them to say rather than face another beating.'

He was also troubled by the crime scenes. 'I saw two of the bodies in situ,' he said, 'and neither of them looked like a gang attack. Both women were huddled in the corners of the rooms with their heads and shoulders sliced to ribbons and defence wounds to their arms. It looked to me as if they were trying to protect themselves from a single individual who attacked from the front. A gang would have been slashing at them from all sides.'

'What can you do?'

'Very little. No one's been interested since the youths confessed. I've written a report, pointing up the anomalies, but there are precious few doctors in Freetown, let alone forensic pathologists.' He smiled ruefully. 'The thinking seems to be that they deserve what they're getting because there's no doubt they were trying to abduct young Amie.'

'If you're right, won't the killer strike again? Won't that exonerate the boys?'

'It depends who he is. If he's a local, then probably . . . but if he's one of the foreign contingent – ' he shrugged – 'I'm guessing he'll export his activities elsewhere.'

I'm sure it was that conversation which increased my suspicions of John Harwood. When he was first pointed out to me in Paddy's Bar (Freetown's equivalent of Stringfellows) I knew I'd seen him before. I wondered if it was in Kinshasa in 1998 when I was covering the civil war in the Congo. I recalled him being in uniform – almost certainly as a mercenary because the British army wasn't involved in that conflict – but I didn't think he'd been calling himself John Harwood.

By the spring of 2002 in Sierra Leone he was dressed in civvies and had a bad reputation. I saw him in three fights while I was there and heard about others, but he was never on the receiving end of the damage. He had the build of a terrier – middling height, lean muscular frame, strong neck and limbs – and a terrier's ferocity once he had his teeth into someone. Most of the ex-pats gave him a wide berth, particularly when he was drinking.

At that time Freetown was full of foreigners. The UN was coordinating efforts to put the country back on its feet, and most of the ex-pats worked for the international press, NGOs, religious missions or world charities. A few, like Harwood, had private contracts. He was employed as chauffeur/bodyguard to a Lebanese businessman, who was rumoured to have interests in a diamond mine. Once in a while the pair of them vanished abroad with heavily armoured cases, so the rumours were probably true.

Along with everyone else, I tended to avoid him. Life was too short to get involved with loners with chips on their shoulders. However, I did make one overture during the six months I was there when I asked him to pass on a request for an interview with his boss. Diamonds were a hot topic in the aftermath of conflict. The question of who owned them and where the money was going had been a bone of contention in Sierra Leone for decades. None of the wealth was fed back into the country and the people's resentment at their grinding, subsistence-level poverty had been a spark of the civil war.

Predictably, I got nowhere near Harwood's boss, but I had a brief exchange with Harwood himself. None of the local women would cook or clean for him, so most evenings he could be found eating alone at Paddy's Bar, which was where I approached him. I said I thought our paths had crossed before and he acknowledged it with a nod.

'You're bonnier than I recall, Ms Burns,' he said in a broad Glaswegian accent. 'Last time I saw you you were a little rat of a thing.'

I was surprised he remembered my name, even more surprised by the backhanded compliment. The one fact everyone knew about Harwood was that he didn't like women. Dislike poured out of him under the influence of Star beer, and gossip had it that he was in the tertiary stage of syphilis after contracting it from a whore. This was a convenient explanation for his aggressive misogyny, but I didn't believe it myself. Penicillin was too freely available for any experienced soldier to progress beyond the primary stage.

I told him what I wanted and placed a list of questions on the table, together with a covering letter explaining the nature of the piece I was planning. 'Will you pass these on to your boss and give me his answer?' Access to anyone was difficult except through a third party. The rebel fighters had destroyed most of the communications network and, with everyone living in secure compounds, it was impossible to blag your way past the guards without an appointment.

Harwood prodded the papers back at me. 'No to both questions.'

'Why not?'

'He doesn't talk to journalists.'

'Is that him speaking or you?'

'No comment.'

I smiled slightly. 'So how do I get past you, Mr Harwood?'

'You don't.' He crossed his arms and stared up at me through narrowed eyes. 'Don't push your luck, Ms Burns. You've had your answer.'

My dismissal, too, I thought wryly. Even with a score of ex-pats within hailing distance, I didn't have the nerve to press him further. I'd seen the kind of damage he could do and I didn't fancy being on the receiving end.

Paddy's was the favoured watering hole of the international community because it remained open throughout the eleven-year conflict. It was a large, open-sided bar-cum-restaurant, with tables on a concrete veranda and it was a magnet for local hookers in search of dollars. They learnt very quickly to avoid Harwood after he hurt one so badly that she was hospitalized. He spoke pidgin English, which is the lingua franca of Sierra Leone, and cursed the girls vilely if they tried to approach him. He called them 'devils' feathers' and lashed out with his fists if they came too close. It reinforced the rumours of whore-induced syphilis, and explained why none of the local girls wanted to work for him.

He was rather more careful around Europeans. The charities and missions had a high percentage of female staff, but if a white woman jogged his arm he always let it go. Perhaps he was intimidated by them – they were a great deal brighter than he was, with strings of letters after their names – or perhaps he knew he wouldn't be able to get away with it. The less articulate black girls were too frightened to lay charges. His attitude persuaded most of us that he was a racist as well as a woman-hater.

There was no telling how old he was. He had a shaven head tattooed with a winged scimitar at the base of his skull, and the sun had dried his skin to leather. When drunk, he boasted that he'd been in the SAS unit that stormed the Iranian embassy in London in 1980 and the scimitar was his badge of honour to prove it. But, if true, that would have put him in his late forties or early fifties and his devastating punches suggested he was younger. Despite the strong Scottish accent, he claimed to come from London, although no one in the UK ex-pat community believed him, any more than they believed that John Harwood was the name he was born with.

Nevertheless, if Alan Collins hadn't made his remark about the foreign contingent, it wouldn't have occurred to me that there might be more to Harwood's violence than anyone realized. Even when it did, there was nothing I could do. Alan had returned to Manchester by then and the murders of the women had quickly faded from the collective memory.

I ran my suspicions past a few of my colleagues, but they were sceptical. As they pointed out, the killings had stopped with the arrest of the boys, and Harwood's modus operandi was to use his fists, not a machete. The tenor of their argument seemed to be that, however despicable Harwood was, he wouldn't have raped the women before murdering them. 'He can't even bring himself to *touch* a black,' said an Australian cameraman, 'so he's hardly likely to soil himself by dipping his wick into one.'

I gave up because the only evidence I could cite against Harwood was the particularly brutal attack on the young prostitute in Paddy's Bar. A good hundred people had witnessed it, but the girl had taken money in lieu of prosecution so there wasn't even a report of the incident. In any case, my stint in Sierra Leone was almost at an end and I didn't want to start something that might delay my departure. I persuaded myself it wasn't my responsibility and confined justice to the dustbin of apathy.

By then I'd spent most of my life in Africa, first as a child, then working for newspapers in Kenya and South Africa, and latterly for Reuters as a newswire correspondent. It was a continent I knew and loved, having grown up in Zimbabwe as the daughter of a white farmer, but by the summer of 2002 I'd had enough. I'd covered too many forgotten conflicts and too many stories of financial corruption. I planned to stay for a couple of months in London, where my parents had been living since 2001, before moving on to the Reuters' bureau in Singapore to write about Asian affairs.

The night before I left Freetown for good, I was in the middle of packing when Harwood came to my compound. He was escorted to my door by Manu, one of the Leonean gate-guards, who knew enough about the man's reputation to ask if I wanted a chaperone. I shook my head, but protected myself by talking to Harwood on my veranda in full view of the rest of the compound.

He studied my unresponsive expression. 'You don't like me much, do you, Ms Burns?'

'I don't like you at all, Mr Harwood.'

He looked amused. 'Because I wouldn't pass on your request for an interview?'

'No.'

The one-word response seemed to throw him. 'You shouldn't believe everything people say about me.'

'I don't have to. I've seen you in action.'

A closed expression settled on his face. 'Then you'll know not to cross me,' he said.

'I wouldn't bet on it. What do you want?'

He showed me an envelope and asked me to mail it in London, a common request to anyone going home because the Leonean postal service was notoriously unreliable. The usual routine was to leave the package open so that the bearer could show Customs at both ends that there was nothing illegal in it, but Harwood had sealed his. When I refused to accept it unless he was prepared to reveal the contents, he returned the envelope to his pocket.

'You'll be needing a good turn from me one day,' he said.

'I doubt it.'

'If you do, you won't get it, Ms Burns. I have a long memory.'

'I don't expect to meet you again, so the situation won't arise.'

He turned away. 'I wouldn't bet on it,' he said in ironic echo. 'For people like us the world's smaller than you think.'

As I watched him walk to the gate, I was curious about the name I'd glimpsed on the envelope, Mary MacKenzie, and the last line of the address, Glasgow. It flipped a switch in my memory. It *was* Kinshasa where I'd seen him before – he was part of a mercenary group fighting for Laurent Kabila's regime – and the name he'd been using was Keith MacKenzie.

I must have wondered why he'd assumed an alias, and how he'd acquired a passport as John Harwood, but it wouldn't have been for long. I spoke the truth when I said I didn't expect to meet him again.

# Two

Two years later, in the spring of 2004, I recognized Harwood immediately. I was on a three-month secondment to Baghdad to cover the rapidly deteriorating situation in Iraq, which was about as long as any newswire journalist could take the stress of the unfolding shambles. Editors around the world were demanding instant copy since the publication of photographs showing US soldiers abusing prisoners in Abu Ghraib jail.

It was a dangerous time for Westerners. Civilian contractors were being targeted for hostage-taking and execution, and private security firms were recruiting ex-soldiers by the thousand to bodyguard them. Iraq had become a bonanza for mercenaries. They were paid double what they could earn anywhere else, but the risks were enormous. Shoot-outs between private security agents and Iraqi insurgents were common, but they rarely hit the headlines. Discreet veils were drawn over the incidents to protect client confidentiality, for as often as not the client was the US government.

In the wake of the Abu Ghraib scandal, with the

coalition lurching from one public relations' disaster to another, a charm offensive was launched to mitigate the damage done by the 'torture' photographs. This involved bussing the press corps to different types of detention and training facilities with promises of full and free access. Being cynical hacks, few of us expected to hear anything that wasn't 'on message', but we went along for the rides just to escape the claustrophobia of our fortress hotels.

There was no venturing out on the streets of Iraq alone at that time, not if we valued our lives and freedom. With an al-Qaeda bounty on every Western head – and women being targeted as potential 'sex slaves' after Lynndie England's part in the prisoner abuse – press accreditation was no protection. Baghdad had been dubbed the most dangerous city in the world and, rightly or wrongly, women journalists saw rapists round every corner.

One of these PR tours ended at the police academy, where they were pushing out five hundred newly trained Iraqi policemen every two months. The coalition authorities had briefed their people well and we received the same human rights' spiel at the academy as we'd heard everywhere else. The buzz phrases of the moment were: 'in accordance with the law', 'clarified chains of command', 'absolute commitment to humanitarian principles', 'proper checks and balances'.

They were fine-sounding sentiments and honestly meant by the smart young Iraqi who pronounced them, but they were no more likely to prevent future abuse than the Nazi Nuremberg trials or the inquiry into the My Lai massacre in Vietnam. If I'd learnt anything from my forays into the world's conflicts, it was that sadists exist everywhere and war is their theatre.

Thoroughly bored, I glanced through an open office window as the press crocodile wound around the main building. In the centre of the room several uniformed dog-handlers, with Alsatians on leashes, faced a man in civvies with his back to me. I'd have known MacKenzie's bullet head anywhere from the winged-scimitar tattoo, but he turned as his listeners' attention was drawn by the voice of our escort and there was no mistaking his face. More out of surprise than any desire to speak to him, I came to a halt, but if he recognized me he gave no sign of it. With an impatient scowl, he reached for the handle and jerked the window shut.

I caught up with the guide and asked him about the civilian with the shaven head. Who was he and where did he fit into the chain of command? Was he training Iraqis to handle dogs? What were his qualifications? The guide didn't know, but said he'd find out before I left.

Half an hour later I learnt that MacKenzie was now calling himself Kenneth O'Connell and was a consultant with the Baycombe Group – a private security firm that was providing specialist training at the academy. When I requested an interview, I was informed O'Connell was no longer on the premises. I was given a phone number to call the next day. As I made a note of it, I asked the Iraqi what O'Connell's speciality was. Control and restraint techniques, he told me.

The phone number turned out to be the Baycombe Group's main office, which was inside a fortified compound near the bombed-out United Nations headquarters. I was given the run-around when I asked for an interview with O'Connell, and it took a further week to set up a general interview with BG's spokesman, Alastair Surtees. I assumed Mackenzie was making his point about 'good turns' and, if so, I was supremely indifferent to it. In terms of what I planned to write – a hard-hitting piece on the calibre of personnel these firms were recruiting – I expected Surtees to be a lot more forthcoming than a Glaswegian bully who changed names whenever it suited him.

I was wrong. Surtees was urbane and courteous, and as tight as a drum when it came to giving information. He told me he was ex-British army, forty-one years old, and had reached the rank of major in the Parachute Regiment before deciding to join the private sector. He reminded me that the agreed interview time was thirty minutes, then filled the first twenty with a slick presentation of his firm's history and professionalism.

I learnt very little about BG's sphere of operations in Iraq – other than that they were wide-ranging and almost exclusively concentrated on the protection of civilians – and a great deal about the type of men whom BG recruited. Ex-soldiers and policemen of the highest integrity. Tired of this spin, I asked if I could speak to an individual operative in order to hear his story first hand.

Surtees shook his head. 'We couldn't allow that. It would make him a target.'

'I wouldn't use his real name.'

Another shake of the head. 'I'm sorry.'

'How about Kenneth O'Connell at the police academy? He and I know each other, so I'm sure he'll agree to talk to me. The last time we met was in Sierra Leone . . . the time before in Kinshasa. Will you ask him?'

The request clearly came as no surprise to Surtees. 'In fact I believe your information's out of date, Ms Burns, but I'm happy to check.' He eased a laptop across the desk and punched up information on the screen. 'We did have an O'Connell at the academy, but he was transferred a month ago. I'm afraid you were wrongly advised.'

I shook my head. 'I don't think so. He was there a week ago because I saw him.'

'Are you sure it was Kenneth O'Connell?'

It was such an obvious question that it made me laugh. 'No . . . but it's the name I was given for the man I saw. In Freetown he was calling himself John Harwood, in Kinshasa, Keith MacKenzie.' I lifted an amused eyebrow. 'Which makes me wonder how you can vouch for his integrity. What name did you vet him by? He's had at least three to my knowledge.'

'Then it wasn't O'Connell you saw, Ms Burns. He was wrongly identified to you.' He tapped at his keyboard. 'We have no Harwoods or MacKenzies on our books, so I suspect the man you saw is with another firm.'

I shrugged. 'I asked the academy twice if I could do an interview with him – once that afternoon and again a couple of days later when I got through to their press office. On neither occasion was I told that Kenneth O'Connell wasn't employed there any more . . . which I should have been if he was transferred a month ago.'

Surtees shook his head. 'Then they haven't kept their records up to date. As I'm sure you're aware, everything's fairly chaotic in Baghdad at the moment.' He closed the lid of his laptop. 'We're meticulous about *our* records so you can rely on the information I've just given you.'

I drew a Pinocchio doodle on my notepad so that he could see it. 'Where's O'Connell now? What's he doing?'

'I can't answer that. Company policy re our employees is no different from Reuters. Complete confidentiality. Would you expect anything less?'

'Then talk generally,' I encouraged him. 'What qualifies a man to teach restraint techniques to raw recruits in the most dangerous capital in the world? Knowledge of the law? A long and honourable career with Scotland Yard? A period in the military police, even? He appeared to be instructing dog handlers, so I assume he has experience in that field. What sort of qualities does it need? Patience? A good control of his temper?'

He folded his hands on the table. 'No comment.'

'Why not?'

'Because your questions relate to a specific individual and I've already described the sort of people we recruit.'

I extended Pinocchio's nose. 'You must think very highly of O'Connell, Mr Surtees. He's one of your few employees who's *not* working in the private sector . . . or *wasn't* until a week ago. I'm assuming the coalition only takes consultants with scrupulously clean records.'

'Of course.'

'So you checked O'Connell thoroughly.' Surtees nodded. 'What's his background? Where was he born? Where did he grow up? With a name like that he ought to be Irish.'

'No comment.'

I watched him for a moment. 'When I knew him in Sierra Leone, he said he was in the SAS unit that stormed the Iranian embassy in London. Is that what he told you?'

Surtees shook his head.

'I knew it was a load of baloney,' I said amiably. 'That embassy siege was twenty-four years ago and the unit was chosen for its experience. O'Connell

would be a good fifty now if he'd been one of them
. . . unless the SAS was recruiting teenagers in the late
seventies.'

'I'm not denying or confirming anything, Ms
Burns – ' he tapped his watch – 'and you're running
out of time.'

I turned over a page of my notebook and did a
quick sketch of MacKenzie's feathered scimitar, showing it to Surtees. 'He told one of my colleagues that
the tattoo on the back of his head is a symbolic
interpretation of the SAS winged dagger . . . it's his
personal tribute to a crushing victory over Islamic
fundamentalists. Do you think it's appropriate for a
man who holds views like that to train Iraqi
policemen?'

Surtees shook his head again.

'Meaning what? That he never trained them . . . or
it's not appropriate?'

'Meaning, no comment.' He unbuckled his watch
and laid it on the desk. 'Time's up,' he said.

I tucked my pencil behind my ear and reached
for my kitbag. 'He's working in a sensitive area. Control and restraint techniques are used to immobilize
dangerous or violent suspects, and we've seen some
graphic images of what happens when uneducated
sadists end up in charge of detainees. I'm sure you
recall that dogs were used to terrorize the prisoners at
Abu Ghraib. It may not bother you if we have a repeat
of it – you'll wash your hands of it with some creative
record keeping – but it'll bother me.'

The man smiled slightly. 'I'll leave the creative side to you, Ms Burns. I'm afraid I'm too slow-witted to follow your imaginative leaps from the misidentification of one of our employees to my being personally responsible for what went on in Abu Ghraib.'

'Shame on you,' I said lightly. 'I hoped you had more integrity.' I stuffed my notebook and pencil into my kitbag. 'MacKenzie's a violent man. When he was in Sierra Leone he couldn't restrain himself . . . let alone teach others how to do it. He had a Rhodesian ridgeback patrolling his compound which was even more aggressive than he was. He trained it to kill by throwing stray mongrels at it.'

Surtees stood up and held out his hand. 'Good day,' he said pleasantly. 'If there's anything else I can help you with, feel free to phone.'

I pushed myself to my feet and shook the proffered hand. 'I can't afford the time,' I said equally pleasantly, tossing my card onto the table in front of him. 'That's my mobile number in case you feel like talking to *me*.'

'Why would I want to?'

I rested my kitbag on my hip to fasten the straps. 'MacKenzie broke a drunk's forearm in Freetown. I saw him do it. He took it between his hands and snapped it against his knee like a piece of rotten wood.'

There was a short silence before the man gave a sceptical smile. 'I don't think that's possible, not unless the bone was so brittle that anyone could have done it.'

'He wasn't prosecuted,' I went on, 'because the victim was too frightened to report him to the police . . . but a couple of paratroopers – *your* regiment – forced him to pay hefty compensation. You don't get broken bones set for free in Sierra Leone . . . and you sure as hell don't get benefit if you can't work.' I shook my head. 'The man's a sadist and all the ex-pats knew it. He's not the type I'd choose to instruct raw recruits in Baghdad on how to do their jobs properly . . . certainly not in the present climate.'

He stared at me with dislike. 'Is this a personal thing? You seem very intent on destroying a man's reputation.'

'It's certainly a *female* thing,' I told him. 'He has no respect for women.'

He wrote me off as a dyke or a militant feminist and resumed his seat. 'All our operatives are trained in courtesy and respect. Beyond that I can't comment. Goodbye, Ms Burns.'

I walked to the door and flipped the handle with my elbow. 'Just for the record, MacKenzie's victim was a half-starved prostitute who weighed under six stone . . . and I bet she did have brittle bones because every cow in the country had been slaughtered for food by the rebels and calcium-rich milk was a luxury. The poor kid – she was only sixteen years old – was trying to earn money to buy clothes for her baby.

She was tipsy on two beers which another customer had bought her and she jogged MacKenzie's elbow by accident. As retribution, he dislocated hers and fractured her ulna by wrenching her arm open and snapping it backwards across his leg.' I lifted an eyebrow. 'Do you have a comment on that?'

He didn't.

'Have a nice day,' I told him.

In the end I never wrote the piece. I managed to get an interview with a bodyguard from a different security firm, but he'd only recently left the army and Iraq was his first freelance operation. As my original idea had been to show how demand for mercenaries far outweighed supply, with compromises being made in the vetting of recruits if numbers were to be met, a single novice didn't make a story. Also, the public appetite for 'war' stories was wearing thin. All anyone wanted was a solution to the mess, not more reminders that the coalition's grip was slipping.

With the help of a translator, I toured Iraqi newspaper offices and went through three months of back copies, looking for stories about raped and murdered women. Salima, the translator, was sceptical from the outset. 'This is Baghdad,' she told me. 'The only thing anyone's interested in is death by suicide bombing or, better still, acts of sadism on the part of the coalition. Women are raped all the time by husbands they never wanted to marry. Does that count?'

I pointed out that it would take twice as long if she conducted a running commentary all the way through.

'But you're being naive, Connie. Even assuming a European could get close to an Iraqi woman without being spotted – which I don't believe – who's going to report it? Some parts of Baghdad are so dangerous that the Iraqi journalists won't go into them – it's not as if the bombing and shooting have stopped – so how's the death of a single woman going to grab anyone's attention?'

I knew she was right, so I don't know which of us was more surprised when we came across the first story. It was headlined 'Rape on the Increase' and was a statistical account of how the rape and/or abduction of women had risen from one a month before the war to some twenty-five a month afterwards. Based on a Human Rights Watch report, it pointed to the dangers women face when the moral and ethical bases of society are shattered by war.

'It says that rape was rare under Saddam because it was a capital offence,' Salima told me, 'then suggests it was the disbanding of the police force at the start of the occupation that put women's safety in jeopardy. This will interest you.' She followed the text with her finger. ' "With thugs and bandits running lawless districts, women are forced to cower in their homes for fear of their lives and honour. Disgracefully, this is no protection. Fateha Kassim, a devout young widow, was found raped and murdered in her home last week. Her father, who discovered her body, said it was the work of animals. They destroyed her beauty, he said."' She looked up. 'Is that the kind of thing we're looking for?'

I nodded. 'It sounds like a carbon copy of the Sierra Leone killings.'

'But how could he have got at her?'

'I don't know, but I'm sure it's part of the excitement. If he was in the SAS, he'd have been trained to move around without attracting notice. Perhaps he goes in at night. Alan Collins said the crime scenes in Sierra Leone suggested the women had spent some time with their killer before he took the machete to them.'

The second story, the only other one we found, was from a different newspaper, dated a month later. It was buried in the middle pages under the headline 'Mother Dies in Sword Attack', and was very short. Salima translated. ' "The body of Mrs Gufran Zaki was discovered by her son on his return from school yesterday. She was brutally slain by blows and cuts to her head. The attack was described as frenzied. Police are looking for her husband Mr Bashar Zaki, who is said to suffer from depression. Neighbours say he had a sword, which is missing from the house." '

We looked for a follow-up to see if Bashar Zaki had been arrested, but the story had been overtaken by the events at Abu Ghraib jail and there were no further references to it. Nor did the murder of Fateha Kassim feature again. It was difficult to know what to do after that. There was no mileage in the women from an international point of view, so I didn't mention them or my suspicions of MacKenzie to Dan Fry, the Reuters' bureau chief in Baghdad. We were snowed under with more immediate disasters and shortly afterwards Salima, the only other person interested, was sent south to Basra with another correspondent.

More out of frustration than from any real expectation of a response, I unearthed my two pieces from Sierra Leone and had them delivered, along with Salima's translations of the articles on the Baghdad murders and a covering letter, to Alastair Surtees at the Baycombe Group. I also emailed them to Alan Collins via the Greater Manchester Police website. Surtees's only reply was a printed compliments slip, acknowledging receipt of the documents. Alan's, a week later, was rather more encouraging.

'My best suggestion,' he wrote in his email, 'is to contact DI Bill Fraser or DS Dan Williams in Basra. They're doing a similar training job to the one I was doing in Freetown. I've forwarded your email and attachments to Bill Fraser to bring him up to speed, and will add his e-address at the bottom. No guarantees, I'm afraid. If the coalition sectors are acting independently, it will be difficult for Bill to intervene in Baghdad, but he should be able to give you some useful names higher up the chain of command. Meanwhile, be a little wary who you talk to. MacKenzie's inside the loop if he is/has been working with the police, so he'll have no trouble finding out who's accusing him. And even if your suspicions are wrong, you already know he reacts violently when he's crossed.'

His advice came too late. By the time I received it, I'd changed my hotel twice and my bedroom three times in as many days. It's hard to explain how the constant invasion of your space can destroy your equilibrium . . . but it does and it did. The door was always locked when I returned, and nothing was stolen, but the deliberate rearrangement of my possessions frightened me. On one occasion I found my laptop open with my letter to Alastair Surtees onscreen.

I had no proof it was MacKenzie – although I never doubted it – but I couldn't persuade the hotels to take me seriously. It was impossible for a non-resident to enter guests' bedrooms, they said. And what was I complaining about, anyway, when no theft had occurred? It was simply the chambermaid doing her job. My colleagues merely shrugged their shoulders and quoted the 'thief of Baghdad' at me. What else could I expect in this god-awful city?

The only person who might have taken my fears seriously was Dan Fry, but he'd chosen that week to go on R & R in Kuwait. I thought about phoning him and asking if I could transfer to his flat, but I was afraid I'd be even more isolated there than in a hotel full of journalists. There was no point in going to the police. Obsessed with suicide bombers and hostage takers, they wouldn't have given me the time of day. And, in any case, I thought Alan Collins was right. The police were the last people to talk to.

I didn't sleep. Instead I lay awake, clutching a pair of scissors and watching the door with burgeoning paranoia. After four nights I was so exhausted that, when I returned to my room after a press conference to find my knickers with the crotches cut out and my bras soiled with semen, my nerve snapped completely and I applied for immediate sick leave on the grounds of war-induced stress and mental breakdown.

I hadn't spent more than two months in the UK since I left Oxford in 1988, but in Baghdad in the early summer of 2004 all I could dream about was soft summer rain, green grass, narrow hedge-lined lanes, and fields and fields of ripening corn. It was an England I barely knew – drawn as much from fiction and poetry as real life – but it was the safest place I could think of.

I can't imagine why I was so stupid.

## OTHER PAN BOOKS
## AVAILABLE FROM PAN MACMILLAN

All Pan Macmillan titles can be ordered from our website,
www.panmacmillan.com, or from your local bookshop
and are also available by post from:

**Bookpost, PO Box 29, Douglas, Isle of Man IM99 1BQ**
Credit cards accepted. For details:
Telephone: +44 (0)1624 677237
Fax: +44 (0)1624 670923
E-mail: bookshop@enterprise.net
www.bookpost.co.uk

*Free postage and packing in the United Kingdom*

Prices shown above were correct at the time of going to press.
Pan Macmillan reserve the right to show new retail prices on covers
which may differ from those previously advertised in the text
or elsewhere.